Family Meal

Also by Bryan Washington

Memorial

Lot

Family Meal

BRYAN WASHINGTON

RIVERHEAD BOOKS

NEW YORK

2023

RIVERHEAD BOOKS
An imprint of Penguin Random House LLC
penguinrandomhouse.com

Grateful acknowledgment is made for permission to reprint "Bad Mode" © 2022
Sony Music Publishing (Japan) Inc. All rights on behalf of Sony Music Publishing (Japan) Inc.
administered by Sony Music Publishing (US) LLC, 424 Church Street, Suite 1200, Nashville,
TN 37219. All rights reserved. Used by permission.

LIBRARY OF CONGRESS CATALOGING-IN-PUBLICATION DATA

Names: Washington, Bryan, 1993– author.
Title: Family meal : a novel / Bryan Washington.
Description: New York : Riverhead Books, 2023.
Identifiers: LCCN 2023001863 (print) | LCCN 2023001864 (ebook) |
ISBN 9780593421093 (hardcover) | ISBN 9780593421116 (ebook)
Subjects: LCGFT: Novels.
Classification: LCC PS3623.A86737 F36 2023 (print) |
LCC PS3623.A86737 (ebook) | DDC 813/.6—dc23/eng/20230203
LC record available at https://lccn.loc.gov/2023001863
LC ebook record available at https://lccn.loc.gov/2023001864

International edition ISBN: 9780593716168

Printed in the United States of America
1st Printing

Book design by Alexis Farabaugh

For T, A, P, and L

This is a work of fiction that touches on self-harm, disordered eating, and addiction. If you're dealing with mental health struggles or body dysmorphia, then this novel could be taxing for you. So please be kind to yourself. And go at your own pace. There's no wrong way to be, and the only *right* way is the way that *you* are. Care and slowness are two gifts that we deserve, boundless pools we can offer ourselves and those we hold dear.

Thanks for reading. Really.

This is, then, a light tale that becomes heavy.

Alejandro Zambra, *Bonsai*

Here's a diazepam
We can each take half of
Or we can roll one up
However the night flows

"Bad Mode," Utada Hikaru

Flowers return with the seasons.
If only we could, too.

Lucky Chan-sil

Family Meal

Cam

Most guys start pairing off around one, but TJ just sits there sipping his water. Everyone else slinks away from the bar in twos and threes. They're fucked up and bobbing down Fairview, toward somebody's ex-boyfriend's best friend's apartment. Or the bathhouse in midtown. Or even just out to the bar's patio, under our awning, where mosquitoes crash-land into streetlamps until like six in the morning. But tonight, even after we've turned down the music and undimmed the lights and wiped down the counters, TJ doesn't budge. It's like the motherfucker doesn't even recognize me.

For a moment, he's a blank canvas.

A face entirely devoid of our history.

But he wears this grin I've never seen before. His hair tufts out from under his cap, grazing the back of his neck. And he's always been shorter than me, but his cheeks have grown softer, still full of the baby fat that never went away.

I'm an idiot, but I know this is truly a rare thing: to see someone you've known intimately without them seeing you.

It creates an infinitude of possibility.

But then TJ blinks and looks right at me.

Fuck, he says.

Fuck yourself, I say.

Fuck, says TJ. Fuck.

You said that, I say. Wanna drink something stronger?

TJ touches the bottom of his face. Fiddles with his hair. Looks down at his glass.

He says, I didn't even know you were back in Houston.

Alas, I say.

You didn't think to tell me?

It's not a big deal.

Right, says TJ. Sure.

The speakers above us blast a gauzy stream of pop chords, remixed beyond comprehension. Dolly and Jennifer and Whitney. They're everyone's cue to pack up for the night. But guys still lean on the bar top in various states of disarray—a gay bar's weekend cast varies wildly and hourly, from the Mexican otters draped in leather, to the packs of white queers clapping off beat, to the Asian bears lathered in Gucci, to the Black twinks nodding along with the bass by the pool table.

As the crowd finally thins out, TJ grabs his cap, running a hand through his hair. He groans.

Feel free to hit the dance floor, I say.

You know I don't do that shit, says TJ.

Then you really haven't changed. But I'll be done in a minute, if you want to stick around.

Fine, says TJ.

Good, I say, and then I'm back at my job, closing out the register and restocking the Bacardí and turning my back on him once again.

I hadn't heard from TJ in *years.*

We hadn't actually *seen* each other in over a decade.

Growing up, his house stood next door to mine. My folks were rarely around, so TJ's kept an eye on me. I ate at his dinner table beside Jin and Mae. Borrowed his sweaters. Slept beside him in his bed with his breath on my face. When my parents died—in a car accident, clipped by a drunk merging onto I-45, I'd just turned fifteen, cue cellos—his family took me into their lives, gave me time and space and belonging, and for the rest of my life whenever I heard the word *home* their faces beamed to mind like fucking holograms.

Not that it matters now. Didn't change shit for me in the end.

Before I start mopping, Minh and Fern wave me off. When I ask what their deal is, Fern says it's rude to keep suitors waiting.

He seems pretty into you, says Minh.

He isn't, I say.

And he's not your usual type, says Fern. I've never seen you go for cubs.

I'm constantly evolving, I say, but we're not fucking.

Spoken like an actual whore, says Minh.

Fern owns the bar. Minh's his only other employee. After I flick them off, I step outside and it's started to drizzle. And TJ's still standing by the curb, sucking on a vape pen as he taps at his phone, blowing a plume of pot into the air once he spots me. The rain pokes holes through his cloud.

You've lost weight, says TJ.

And you've gained it, I say.

Nice.

It's no shade. You finally look like a baker.

But it's different. You're—

That's what you want to talk about?

It was an observation, says TJ. I have eyes.

Did you park nearby, I ask.

Nah.

Then I'll walk you to your car like a gentleman.

Ha, says TJ, and we drift along the sidewalk, ducking into the neighborhood under stacks of drooping fronds.

· · ·

The middle of Montrose is busted concrete and monstrous greenery and bundled town houses. Scattered laughter bubbles along the roads snaking beside
us, even at this time of night. Bottles break and engines snarl. But TJ's pace is
steady, so I ease mine, too. Sometimes he glances my way, but nothing comes
out of his mouth.

Deeply stimulating conversation, I say.

I don't think you get to be like that with me, says TJ.

Is that right? After all these years?

It's not like I planned on running into you tonight, says TJ. This isn't a date.

So you're actually dating now, I say, instead of fucking straight boys?

Shut *up*, says TJ. How long have you been in Houston? And don't lie.

Relax, I say. Just a few months.

What's a few?

A few since Kai died.

Oh, says TJ.

He stops in the center of a driveway. A gaggle of queens searching for their
Lyft walks around us, whistling at nothing in particular.

Shit, says TJ. Sorry.

Nothing for you to be sorry about, I say.

No, says TJ. Not about that. Or not completely. But I never got to talk to
you, after what happened.

After, I say.

After, says TJ. You know.

He keeps his eyes on the concrete. One of his hands forms a fist.

The reaction's totally human. But it still isn't good enough for me.

So I walk up to TJ, standing closer.

You didn't kill him, I say.

I know, but—

No *but*s. Don't be a fucking downer.

TJ doesn't say anything. He takes another hit of the pen. And he extends it to me, dangling the battery from his fingers, so I take that off his hands and huff a hit of his weed, too.

We walk a few more blocks, hopscotching across Hopkins's sidewalks, toward Whitney and Morgan and the gays honking in Mini Coopers behind us. We pass a pair of Vietnamese guys steadying each other by the shoulders, torn up from their night out, taking care not to step on any cracks. We pass a huddle of drunk bros holding court on a taquería's corner, swinging their phones and laughing way too loudly. When one of them asks if we're looking to party, I feel TJ tense up, so I tell them we're good, maybe next time, and add a little extra bass in my voice.

But the guys just wave us off. TJ and I duck under another set of branches. And then we're alone on the road, again, beyond the neighborhood's gravity of queer bars, where it's as silent as any other white-bread Texas suburb.

Hey, I say. Does showing up at the bar mean you're finally out?

I was always out, says TJ.

Right, I say. But are you—

My car's here, says TJ, nodding at a tiny Hyundai parked by the intersection.

He leans against the door while I fiddle with my pockets. It makes no fucking sense that I'm nervous. But when TJ asks if I need a ride back to my place, I decline, pointing toward the neighborhood.

I'm local, I say.

Of course you are, says TJ.

Staying with a friend. Another friend.

One that knew you were in this fucking city.

TJ speaks plainly, like he's describing the weather.

What the fuck would you have done if I'd told you, I say.

I guess we'll never know, says TJ.

He makes a funny face then. Another one I've never seen before. Something like a smirk.

So I think about what I'm going to say, and I open my mouth to launch it—but then I change my mind.

Because TJ's earned at least this much.

Instead, I reach for his pen, pulling another hit. I blow that back in his face. When TJ waves it away, I blow another.

Listen, he says. Seriously. You're really okay?

It's a short walk, I say.

No. I mean, are *you* all right?

I twirl TJ's pen a few times. He really does look like he means it.

Come back to the bar and see me, I say. I'll be around.

TJ gives me a long look, pursing his lips. Then he reaches into his car, snatching something, pushing it against my chest.

It's a paper bag filled with pastries. Chicken turnovers. They're flaky in my hands, warm to the touch, and the smell sends a chill up my neck—entirely too familiar.

Are you the fucking candy man, I say.

Try them, says TJ.

How do I know they aren't laced?

Because I'd have poisoned you years ago.

So I take a bite of the pastry.

It's just as delicious as I remember.

And when TJ sees my face, he nods.

Then he steps into his car without glancing my way, and I watch him drive off, and I wait for him to wave or throw a peace sign or whatever the fuck but he doesn't. TJ turns the corner and he's gone.

So I take another bite of the turnover, tasting the food, rolling it around my mouth.

Then I spit it out.

It's only another block before I find a trash can to dump the rest.

. . .

A few streets later, my phone pings from one of the apps. The message's sender drops his location. This park's tucked a couple of blocks away. But the guy doesn't send a photo of his face, just his dick, and I'm not entirely sure who I'm supposed to be looking for.

Cruising's a nightmare this way. You always risk running into some fucking homophobe. Or bored frat kids looking to blow off steam with a baseball bat. Or a drunk married dick with twelve kids and a lovely, clueless wife. But eventually, I spot a dude sitting on this bench beside a playground, and I recognize him immediately: it's one of the bros we passed at the taquería.

He looks shook at the sight of me. Late thirties, early forties. When I'm close enough, this guy sticks out his hand for a shake, and when I tell him to calm the fuck down, he apologizes, blushing.

I wonder how drunk he is.

Or what it took for him to work up to this point.

But I let him bend me over anyway.

He fucks me on the bench. Our motions feel routine, like they're untapped muscle memory—and it reminds me of something Kai liked to say, about how the steps may be the same, but we each have our own particular rhythm, and this was just another one of his nonsense manifestos but I still haven't forgotten it—and that's what comes to mind as this stranger stuffs one hand in my shirt while his other one plays with my ass, searching for an angle.

But it isn't long before we start to stall.

I reach for the guy's dick, guiding him, and he grabs my wrist.

Wait, he says. Do you have a condom?

No, I say. You're fine.

Really?

Go for it.

You're sure?

Are you a fucking doctor?

And I'm thinking that this guy will ask a fiftieth time but he doesn't. He enters me slowly. Starts pumping his hips tentatively. And then quickly. I steady myself on the wood, buckling from our momentum, thinking of how I'll probably find someone else to fuck after this, until, all of a sudden, I hear Kai's voice, clear as day, and I'm pushing his face from my mind while the guy behind me grunts under his breath—and when he comes, our bodies jolt, and I almost start to laugh because it's fucking hilarious and nothing short of astounding that I thought the world could ever be anything but what it is or that I'd ever truly find myself outside of its whims.

A while back, Kai asked about TJ. We lived in LA. I still had my bank gig. Kai worked as a translator, and he still looked at me in a bewildered way, like he couldn't believe our luck, as if the fact of our finding each other was such a fucking miracle. He liked hanging out in the park a few blocks from his apartment in Silver Lake, despite the tents and the drunks and the sugar babies snapping photos under the roses, and a few years into our situation this was a thing that hadn't changed.

So I started joining him.

Not always. But occasionally.

On the way over, Kai grabbed lemonades from this tiny Japanese convenience store. The owners knew his name. They'd talk about Kansai, which is where Kai flew every few months for work, and also the food and the cherry blossoms and whatever the fuck else and the sight never failed to confuse everyone in line: a lumpy Black dude chatting with these hundred-year-old Asians about the way that snow falls halfway across the world. I didn't get it either.

But then we'd split from the shop, sprawling across the park's grass, shutting our eyes to the tune of toddlers and traffic. Kai liked saying that you'd never find this in Louisiana, where he'd grown up, as if I didn't already fucking know that.

Houston's the same, I said. You get your concrete and your brown and that's it.

You're exaggerating, said Kai.

I wouldn't be paying a brick to live here otherwise.

What about that one friend back home?

Who?

The only one you've ever mentioned, said Kai.

He reached into the plastic bag between us, flicking a cherry tomato at my face. I caught it with my mouth. Some Black women in shades formed a yoga circle beside us, working their bodies into the lotus position. Every few minutes, their group burst into laughter, sending ripples through the park.

There's nothing to tell, I said. TJ and I grew up together. His folks owned a bakery. I worked there until college, and then I left, and TJ got weird. His dad died a few years later. You know most of this already.

But you could be more generous, said Kai.

Maybe, I said. But that's life. I grew up with his old man, too. I didn't freak out when he passed.

Kai's eyes flickered. The women beside us raised their arms, working their way up toward the warrior pose.

Thank you, I said.

For what, said Kai.

For not saying that he wasn't really family.

Now you're being silly, said Kai. What's TJ doing now?

Nothing, I said. Stuck at the bakery. Dating closet cases.

Hey, said Kai, sitting up. There's no clock for coming out. No one way to be queer.

Word. But it's different.

How?

Kai bit another mouthful of sandwich. The women beside us released their stances, exhaling and settling back onto their mats. And I thought about Kai's question, but I couldn't come up with an answer.

Or whatever answer for TJ's situation I conjured felt like it'd take too fucking long to explain.

So Kai flicked another tomato. This one hit me in the eye.

Fucker, I said.

You're spacing out, said Kai.

I'm thinking.

That's cute. Did you and TJ ever fool around?

Please.

It'd be natural! You were teens!

While Kai laughed, I slipped a finger in the hip of his boxers. He pushed at my chest with his palm. It was enough for a few of our neighbors to stare, blinking before they turned back to their huddle.

Anyways, I said. We fell out of touch. The end.

But you loved him, said Kai.

Did I say that?

You didn't have to, said Kai. It's on your face.

Is that right?

Yeah, babe. That's love.

And then Kai crossed his eyes, sticking his tongue out and shaking his head.

I meant to ask Kai what he'd seen in me.

What love looked like to him.

It was a stupid fucking question and I never got around to it.

And then, obviously, he died.

But sometimes I still talk to him.

Still don't know how it happens.
Or why.

Sometimes there's a warning.

Like I'll get this fucking chill in my neck.

But, mostly, Kai just shows up.

I'll be in the shower, or taking a piss, or just about to nod off, and then, poof. He'll appear. Sitting cross-legged right in front of my fucking face.

The last time it happened was a few weeks back. I was in bed, alone, tapping at my phone. Looking for dick. And then, out of the fucking blue, I felt Kai on the mattress beside me.

We lay there in silence. With me breathing up all the air and him being dead and still.

And then Kai burped.

I said, Fuck.

That's cute, said Kai. It's been a while.

I didn't ask Kai where he'd been.

Or what the fuck he was doing now.

Because he was *there.* As sure as I was.

But he was also gone.

And he'd *been* gone.

You've been busy, said Kai.

I was making moves, I said. Reorganizing my life.

You make it sound so easy.

It's slower in Texas. You like slow things.

Liked, said Kai.

Yeah, I said, sorry.

You're apologetic now, said Kai. Don't start being decent on my account.

It's not like you tried to change me.

Why would I? Romance with qualifications is just a crush.

But there's less room for that kind of trouble here, I said.

Where the fuck is *here*?

Wherever you aren't, I said.

You know that's bullshit, said Kai. Trouble's always around if you know where to look.

You weren't looking for me, I said, and you found trouble.

We don't always get it right, said Kai.

Then did you regret it, I thought, but I didn't say the words, and Kai sneezed so loudly that I jolted.

He said, Things are different now. I'm the only one who gets to ask questions, okay?

And then he was gone again.

Just like that.

Like a little bitch.

Our bar's called Harry's and Minh spells that with an *i*. Fern inherited the property. He says the place was named after some innovative white man, who allegedly unified the neighborhood against other marginally more racist white men, but whenever Fern tells that story he starts laughing halfway through so I can never tell if he's bullshitting or what.

The building sits on a shrubby curb of Montrose. It's hidden under too many pine cones. Houston is shit for seasons, so the neighborhood stays inexplicably green year-round. The block itself was patchworked from a hodgepodge of estates, alongside a bunch of half-built condos, and evergreens, and the occasional upper-middle-class assemblage of curated flowers planted by homeowners who'd scarfed up property before the housing loophole closed. It's beautiful garbage.

But the bar's always in danger of closing. Fern bitches about this daily. Not that he needs to—the queer bookstore and the queer grocery store and the queer sex store and the lesbian tailors and the queer coffee shops just beyond our bubble are already gone. Their buildings got bulldozed. Or they were priced out. And now, between the construction fences, we've got signs advertising high-rises and boutique strip malls named after even more white men whose great-grandfathers probably owned slaves.

Sometimes they're splattered with graffiti. But it's only like a day before they're wiped clean with fresh coats of paint.

Fern set me up with the bar gig. He'd known Kai in LA. They'd met at some fucking nerd convention, because Fern's husband read this book Kai had translated and they'd all stayed in touch. Which was yet another pocket of Kai's life that I hadn't been privy to—but then Fern called me a few weeks after the funeral in Louisiana.

Which I hadn't gone to.

But I wasn't invited.

The job's nothing fancy, said Fern, and the pay's pretty shit. But you'll be around people you won't have to explain anything to.

I took the call on our balcony. I hadn't really been going outside. Hadn't really been getting dressed. In the mornings, I watched daylight hit the road from our bedroom window. In the evenings, I watched the sun set from our kitchen. Sometimes, around midnight, I'd slip out to Melrose for tacos, or I'd splurge on dim sum delivered from downtown, ordering enough stir-fried noodles and BBQ buns for six.

Sometimes I ate everything.

Although I mostly didn't.

I don't know, I told Fern. Houston's far. And I don't love Texas.

Didn't you grow up around here, asked Fern.

How do you know that, I said, and I listened to Fern breathe on the phone, because I wanted to see if he'd dare to say Kai's name but he didn't.

Look, said Fern. There's no pressure. It's your choice. But a change of scenery might do you good. Even if it's only for a little while.

I don't think you know me well enough to say that.

I know you've lost someone. I know you're grieving. And I know Los Angeles is probably the last place you want to be right now. Given, you know, all of it.

Doesn't matter either way, I said. I wouldn't even have a place to sleep.

You can stay with me.

What? Why the fuck are you doing this?

Don't worry about that, said Fern.

Then he added: We loved Kai, too. He talked about you all the time.

I started to say, He never mentioned you—but I didn't.

My toes bent into the tile instead.

TJ called, too.

Week after week. A few times every day.

I let his messages run straight to my voice mail until it was finally full. Never felt the need to listen.

But when TJ's mother called, I answered.

We were silent on the phone until Mae said my name. She asked how I was doing, and if I was eating, and if I had money. She didn't bring up Kai even once, but I couldn't make myself hate her for it.

If you need anything, said Mae, you know where to find us.

Thanks, Mae.

Our home is still your home, too.

Thanks, Mae.

Whenever you need to come by, she said, there's a place for you here.

I don't think I can do that, I said.

There was a pause on the line. I could hear the words before she spoke them.

That's all right, said Mae. As long as you know that you can change your mind.

The very next morning, I called Fern back.

I booked a flight that evening.

Made it a one-way ticket.

A few days later, TJ's back at the bar. He fingers his phone, wincing in the same black hoodie. And if he sees me, he doesn't let on.

He nearly has the place to himself. Weekday traffic doesn't keep us afloat. A Black guy in a ball cap sits at one end of the counter, stirring his cocktail. A pair of Filipino gays giggle just under the television, drowned out by the sounds of Janet Jackson. And a Venezuelan dude frowns at his phone, glancing continually at the entrance, until I ask if he's expecting anyone and he says they'll be here any minute.

Eventually, Minh calls me over from the register. He's taking stock of the liquor with Fern, docking everything on a tablet. Business is slow enough for him to lodge an ASL textbook under the counter—Minh's been studying speech pathology on and off, and he swears this is the year that he'll finish.

Your trade is back, he says.

You're projecting, I say.

Maybe, says Minh. Is he mixed?

His dad's Korean, I say. Mom's Black.

I think he really is just a friend, says Fern.

No one asked you, says Minh.

I've got an eye for these things, says Fern. And baby boy would've told us if he had a paramour, right?

Absolutely not, I say. Can you cover the bar for a bit?

Is this a favor, says Minh.

If that means you'll do it.

Then it's my pleasure, says Minh, waving his palms in a flourish.

That makes Fern grunt. But he can't do shit about it. And it's not like all of us need to hang around by the register anyway. Like every other gay bar that's survived, we're held hostage by Saturdays. Between theme nights and game nights and holidays, most of our revenue arrives in lump sums, and since Fern's sworn off hosting circuit parties we're rarely an event planner's primary choice.

Fern assures us rent isn't an issue. Swears he'll remortgage his house before he drops us from payroll. But Minh told me he's seen our landlord around more often lately, although I never seem to catch her myself.

When I asked Fern about this a few weeks back, he narrowed his eyes.

So now you want to balance the books, he said.

I just don't want to end up on the street, I said.

You won't, said Fern. I'm handling it.

It was the gruffest he'd ever been with me.

But now, taking the seat beside TJ, the amount of people in here is hardly reassuring. Our other patrons are stuck in their own tiny constellations. When the door behind us opens, the Venezuelan dude jolts, but a flinty voice calls out *Sorry, honey* before it slams again.

So, I say.

You thought I wouldn't show, says TJ.

When I said to come back, I didn't mean on your lunch break.

Too bad, says TJ. I brought a message from Mae.

How's she doing?

Ask her yourself. It's been years.

We talked a few months ago, I say, which is enough for TJ to finally look up.

He sips from his glass—another fucking water—before clearing his throat.

Okay, Viola Davis, I say. Don't be dramatic.

Fuck you, says TJ.

You wish. And it's not like we talked shit about you. She was just looking out.

I don't care.

You know we've always been close, I say. You and Jin would disappear wherever, and she'd hang back with me.

But apparently not close enough for you to drop by when you got to town, says TJ. She wants to see you in person. Couldn't believe it when I said you were back.

You told her you ran into me at a gay bar?

TJ wipes his nose at this.

The baby gays sitting under our television yelp. When we glance their way, they're laughing into their hands, rocking their table and spilling beer all over the tile. Minh glides over with a towel, shaking his head, and they apologize between spurts of giggling.

How are things at the bakery, I say.

We're still around, says TJ.

That's good.

You didn't have to leave.

That isn't what we're talking about today, I say.

I just wanted you to hear it from me, says TJ. In case you'd forgotten.

You don't get to do that.

I'm just saying.

Then stop, I say. What the fuck are you even doing here?

You told me to come back, says TJ.

That's all it took?

I'm not the one who left.

It suddenly occurs to me that we're yelling. Fern and Minh gawk our way. Everyone else is staring right along with them.

The stereo dips into a glossy city pop. Anri's voice blankets the entire bar. And TJ crosses his arms, leaning against the counter.

Let's drop it, he says. I didn't drive across town to argue.

So you're just here to pick up ass on a Wednesday afternoon?

I thought I was being a friend.

You've done a phenomenal job, I say. A-plus-plus-plus.

TJ lifts his water, downing the rest of it. But as he stands, his barstool tumbles, and I catch his shoulders before he slips.

Which leaves us holding each other.

Looking entirely out of sorts.

You know what, says TJ, *fuck* you.

And then he's out the door. Slamming it behind him.

Fern and Minh start clapping. The boys by the television shake their heads, resuming their flirt. And the Black guy lost in his vodka soda raises a glass my way, but I tell him to fuck right off.

Fern's place sits a few blocks from the bar. It's a single-story three-bedroom, flanked by a laundromat and a Guadalajaran bakery. He lives with Jake—the husband—and sometimes his son passes through during the week, unless Diego's staying with his mom out in midtown.

Jake works mornings as a nurse at an urgent care clinic. Fern works nights at the bar. The first few months, I tried goading them into letting me find another job, or at least to pitch in on groceries, but they wouldn't have it.

It's part of our arrangement: Fern refuses everything from me but my third of the utilities. Which is basically nothing compared to LA. They own their fucking house. So I told Fern that wasn't fair—I still had some savings from when I worked at the bank—and Fern told me *life* wasn't fair, and this was the argument we rehashed every evening, but one night Jake spoke up and said he'd heard I used to work in a bakery, so maybe I could cook for the three of them?

Not happening, I said.

Totally understandable, said Jake.

Wait a minute, said Fern. That's actually not a bad idea.

I said I want to *pay* you.

Then think of this as another kind of transaction, said Fern.

I don't fucking cook anymore, I said. That was a long fucking time ago.

We aren't picky, said Jake, and I started to protest again, but Fern only told me to think about it since I was the one who'd brought this shit up in the first place.

Now I hand Fern a plate with scrambled eggs smothered in Cholula, flanked by a slice of bacon. We've just made it back from the bar. He breaks the yolks with his fork, inhaling the entire plate.

Jesus, I say. Stop that shit or you'll choke.

Would you cry, says Fern.

For days. You really think there's nothing to worry about with Harry's?

There's always something to worry about, says Fern. But we're safe. I promise.

I start to say something else, but I catch myself.

Fern folds his arms on the countertop, resting his elbows. He never really grows his mustache, but a layer of fuzz creeps above his lips.

I'm not putting you out on the street, says Fern. You worry too much.

I worry precisely the correct amount.

And look where it's gotten you, says Fern.

But there's no malice in his voice. Fern finishes the food, carrying his dish to the sink. Then he waves me away, slinking down the hallway, back to bed, while Diego leapfrogs down the stairs with his backpack, juggling a violin case in one hand and a jacket in the other.

The middle school's only a few blocks away, but Fern insists that Diego be walked. And I get where he's coming from. Working in Montrose, we know just how much is possible on these streets, even with the neighborhood's changes. Lately, it's all ice-cream parlors and pop-up boutiques and twelve-dollar coffees on overgrown patios—but a few years back, you wouldn't catch white boomers walking down Fairview or Dunlavy or Hazard in broad day for anything.

Still though—you never fucking know.

And also, Diego has asthma.

So this is another part of my days: cooking everyone breakfast and baby-sitting the kid on his way to school.

But Diego still sulks from block to block, chattering about who has a crush on who, or which YouTuber he's sick of, or connecting the choruses of one K-pop track to another, mostly jabbering to himself, until he looks up at me expecting a response.

You could at least pretend to care, he says.

I'm the prime minister of caring, I say.

Then I should throw a coup.

There's an idea. The people would thank you.

Nah, says Diego. You're too much of a pushover. It'd be too easy.

Diego's a short little guy. He's Fern's kid from his first marriage. Jake does Diego's haircuts, and they're generally good enough, but somehow his hair always ends up looking like he's just parachuted from a fighter jet.

Our walk's decent though: the neighborhood's still recovering from the night before. A handful of white moms fawn on coffee-shop benches. Barbers and clerks unlock their shops lining Westheimer. And when we make it to his school's gates, Diego takes a breath.

You don't have to wait for me this afternoon, he says.

You know that's not how this works, I say.

I know. Just not today.

Is something special happening?

No.

Got a cute date?

No.

What's their name? What're their pronouns?

Stop, says Diego. It's not like that. I just think we should change things up.

Mm, I say. Let me ask your dads how they feel about that.

I already did.

Sure. But let me ask them myself.

Diego squints. He raises his fist toward me, and I bump it, before he lets his hand explode, spinning and sprinting toward the school's steps. He looks back at me before the doors close behind him, flipping me off. But Diego smiles before he's gone.

I check my phone not even eight seconds later and the nearest guy online is like twenty feet away. But I've already fucked him. And he came two minutes in. So I keep swiping, and the distances multiply—from twenty-five feet to fifty to seventy-five to nearly a mile.

Then I get a photo from a faceless profile.

It's some guy smiling with too many teeth.

Cute, I write.

Thanks, he writes. Looking?

depends

?

you a top?

Vers 🙂

that's what everyone says, I write.

For real, writes this guy. Honestly just looking to party.

Interesting, I write. You hosting?

This is my routine: during the day, while Fern sleeps and Jake works, before I head to the bar, I stroll around the neighborhood and these walks are punctuated with sex. Since I've been back in Houston, I've fucked delivery guys and lawyers and dry cleaners and architects and engineers and college kids and kindergarten teachers and graphic designers and real estate agents and salesmen and house husbands and professors. Someone's always just coming home from their gig out in Pearland, or getting ready to leave the gym in Memorial, or out on a jog at Hermann Park, or taking a sick day or sending their kid to school or whatever. But most encounters follow a familiar formula: a rushed introduction before some fucking, until one of us finally comes, and then there's the sprint for the other to finish before we nod and leave, never once exchanging our names and probably never seeing each other again until we pop up on the apps a few days later.

Kai called this the fag tax: perpetual proximity. He swore that we always ended up online, interlinked atoms scattered across a permanent digital grid. I don't know how I got caught up in that, at least to this extent, because of course I fucked around before I met Kai, hooking up here and there, but at some point after he died *here and there* became *everywhere*, all the time, and naming a thing doesn't prevent you from succumbing to it, and when I knock on this guy's door, behind a walk-up complex three blocks from the school, a burly Latinx dude answers.

Hey, I say.

Howdy, he says.

He asks if I want some water. I tell him that's cool if it's bottled. And as he steps off, I look around his place—the pastel walls are full of family photos. A handful seem to have him in them. In one, he's grinning beside a lady who might be his grandmother. In another, he stands arm in arm with three men, looming over a Chihuahua. In every last picture, everyone's beaming, and I wonder if they know he sucks dick.

Is this your place, I ask.

My parents', says the guy. I'm between jobs.

That's cool.

It's cheap. Got let go from a tech contract in Denver, and it just made sense to move back. But I feel like a fucking deadbeat in Texas.

Sounds unbearable, I say.

When this guy makes it back to the living room with two waters, I cheers him.

You have any leads on a job, he asks.

What?

I'm joking, says this guy, and he places a hand on my back.

We jerk each other off in front of his prom portraits. When we amble our way toward the sofa, he asks if I'm cool with fucking him.

Sure, I say, but could we do a line first?

We could, says this guy.

And you're sure it's clean?

I bought it a few years back. Thought I'd save it for a special occasion.

Well then, I say, and this guy gives me a blank look until he finally stands, leaving me in the living room with eighteen photos of his grandmother. When he makes it back, spreading out all of his shit, I take a whiff and instantly feel more like myself.

Wait, I say, you don't want any?

It's a little early, says this guy.

Touché, I say, and that's when we start to kiss.

He asks me to bite his lip. Then he asks me to stroke his balls, and to squeeze his chest, and to finger him faster.

Any other requests, I ask.

Could you be a little rougher?

That's not really my thing.

Okay. But could you try?

So I do. He muffles his moans in the cushions, and I manage to last for twenty minutes. When I tell him I'm coming, he asks me to pull out, and I finish across his back.

Afterward, I sit on the floor while he wipes up the mess beside him. Then this guy sits next to me, downing his water, and he asks for my name.

Um, I say.

That's fine, he says. I get it. But do you want something to eat? Before you go?

I've got lunch plans, I say.

Right, he says.

Except I don't get up right away. And this guy doesn't either. If I'm honest, his openness is jarring—niceness for the sake of niceness doesn't fit into our transaction. But when I finally stand, the guy walks me out, telling me to get home safe.

After I'm maybe a block away, I find him on the app and I block him. We're both better off that way.

When I make it back to the house, Jake's twirling a pair of fried eggs dressed with chopped longganisa. He's in his scrubs, drowsy before his clinic shift in Meyerland.

Don't look so happy to see me, he grins.

Never, I say. Long night?

No longer than usual, says Jake. How was the walk?

Uneventful.

I'm sure, says Jake, chewing a mouthful of yolk.

I hardly ever run into him alone. But I know Jake has family in Alief and Oakland, which is where his folks settled after leaving Manila. I know his brother was a Marine and now he's a stoner amputee. I know his sisters are nurses, just like their mother, and their mother's mother, and that Jake deemed this career the path of least resistance—but whenever I ask Fern how his husband feels about hosting me, he only shakes his head.

Our exchanges usually run all of two minutes. But I've learned little things cooking for Jake the past few months—like how much pepper makes him tear up. And how he can't stomach too many onions. I know how many Modelos make him blush, and how much salt is too much salt, and exactly how firm Jake likes his burger cooked, which is hardly definitive fucking data but it still feels like something.

Fern's snoring seeps down the hall. When he snorts, Jake and I lock eyes, grinning.

We really do appreciate what you're doing, says Jake. I feel like I don't say that enough.

It's literally the bare minimum.

Maybe, says Jake. But that's not nothing.

Well, I say, I'm glad you see it that way.

I really do. You gonna stay up for a bit?

Nah. You've made my job easy.

Jake stands, pouring more coffee into his thermos. He sets a hand on my shoulder as he passes through the door. And I wait until his car starts, pulling out of the lot, but then I sit for another minute just to make sure he's actually gone.

I never asked Kai about his friends back home. And he never volunteered anything. So I just assumed that he was like me: there were important people in his life, but none of them were essential to our story.

Kai grew up in Baton Rouge. I lived in Galveston until my parents pushed over to Houston. Sometimes, in Echo Park, we'd walk the streets surrounding our apartment, toward the knotty shops lined up along Sunset, under the condos peering above them from Glendale, comparing the passersby and the traffic and the blatant faggotry to our situations back home. It was all new to both of us. Which felt like a fucking miracle.

One morning, in our early days, we'd just finished fucking and Kai asked about my childhood home. We stood in his kitchen in our boxers. The window's sheen glowed on our backs. Kai arranged some flowers he'd bought from a street vendor the night before, peeling leaves and trimming stems. His mother grew all sorts of shit in Louisiana, and this was a habit he'd kept from her, one of the few things he'd said about his life in the South.

I love the beach, said Kai, rinsing his hands. But I've never visited one in Texas.

You haven't missed anything, I said.

Is that your famous optimism?

It isn't. Galveston's gross. You had pools in Baton Rouge.

White people have pools and lakes in Baton Rouge.

Then they're not so different.

Give me the chance to decide for myself, said Kai.

I cracked eggs into a handful of bowls. Stirred them with a fork. Kai rarely cooked, but he knew his way around a kitchen: rice buried in nori, or omelets rolled in a square pan. His fridge was hardly ever stocked, because he spent so much time out of town, but Kai still had flour and butter and milk and I threw together a simple dough, molding it across the counter.

He eyed me, drawing circles with his finger.

You're pretty good at that, said Kai.

I'm really not, I said.

Just take the compliment. You're better than me.

That's a low fucking bar.

And you were doing so well about being nice.

I didn't know I was being graded, I said.

But you should've, said Kai.

I twisted the dough with my hands, letting it breathe, separating the mass into chunks and popping the baking tray in the freezer. Kai slid from his edge of the kitchen, skimming his feet across the tile. Leaning against the fridge, he wrapped his arms around my waist, fondling me, and the hair on his legs brushed the backs of my thighs.

We're doing this in here?

Tell me more about this bakery.

Kai slipped a hand in my shorts, and his pulling gained speed. I felt him grow hard behind me.

I made this shit for years, I said. It's all TJ and I did with his dad. I'd be at their place after school every day, just folding croissants and pastries.

Sounds like a nice skill to have, said Kai.

It's what I thought I'd end up doing with my life, I said.

Kai's motions slowed, and I groaned. I felt him laugh behind me, spreading his legs, dropping our boxers, sticking some of himself inside me.

My mom baked every Sunday morning, said Kai. She had a custard pudding recipe that she'd gotten from *her* mom. We never bought dessert because it never came close to hers.

You ever try making it, I said.

Of course. It's our one family thing.

Think you'll ever bake one for me?

You've got a ways to go, said Kai. But what took you out of the kitchen? Did something happen?

Just the same thing that always happens, I said. Fuck, man.

Kai kept pulling and pushing. I told him I'd come if he didn't stop. And Kai said, Then come, so I groaned and I did. Kai laughed, making a triumphant face, but it disappeared as I turned around to face him, rubbing until he moaned and finished, too, and then we washed our hands before he cleaned up the rest of our mess.

I pulled the dough out of the freezer. Popped each wad into the oven. And Kai stood beside me, close enough that I could chew on his shoulder.

He said, Fuck.

What?

If you'd stayed in Texas then you would've never met me out here.

Not necessarily, I said. Maybe you'd have visited Houston. It's not that far from Louisiana.

Maybe, said Kai. But probably not.

Yeah, I said. Probably not.

We fucked again while the biscuits baked. As the timer chimed, Kai asked if we should stop. And I told him to finish, again, and we did, but I still waddled toward the oven with a mitt while Kai hobbled behind me.

Six crisp squares stood on the pan.

The smell nearly knocked me over.

Jesus, said Kai. These look delicious.

They're burnt, I said.

They're beautiful.

You're just being nice.

No, said Kai. They didn't exist before, and you made something from nothing with your own hands. That's a beautiful thing.

Then Kai reached for a biscuit. I set my hand on his chest.

We stood like that for a moment until I reached toward the pan, too.

Lately, that memory's lost its sheen.

We were two fags in an apartment chewing a pair of burnt biscuits.

Stupid stupid stupid stupid stupid, says Kai.

I'm washing dishes at Fern's place. Kai's kicking his legs against the back of the sink. When I see him nowadays, he's always in Sanrio tank tops. Or barefoot in basketball shorts. The sort of shit he never wore in actual life.

Of all the things that happened with us, says Kai, you pick the dumbest one of all to remember.

He holds his hand under the water, flicking drops into my face.

When I flinch, he stops short.

When I don't, he continues to flick.

But it's important to me, I say. You never talked about yourself like that. I had to pull teeth to learn anything about where you came from.

Which makes it even dumber, says Kai, flicking more droplets into my face.

I start to ask what he means, and then I look up and he's gone.

Over the weekend, we schedule a block party for the bar. Fern doesn't seem stressed about it, but he admits that this is one we need to nail.

We'll have a guest of honor, he says. A highly esteemed community figure.

Beyoncé, I say.

No, says Fern.

Solange, says Minh. Or the Astros.

That's an entire team, I say.

Whatever, says Minh. An Astro.

Even better, says Fern. Our landlord.

For a little while, our bar's mostly packed. We've got the pockets of gays who arrived together, and the gays who're trying to leave together, and also some straight white women touring the gayborhood. Minh's haggling with the DJ over his playlists. Fern's mixing cocktails beside me, cackling with some older dudes in Spanish. When one of the men points at me, Fern simply shakes his head. They point again, nodding, insisting on something.

Are they looking for a sugar baby, I ask.

Don't worry about it, says Fern.

Then what is it, I say.

No te preocupes. Es nada.

Don't fucking lie.

Shit, says Fern. They say they recognize you. From the news. But they can't place where.

The two men nod at this.

I open my mouth, and then I close it.

There's a question in Fern's eyes, and I answer it silently.

So I told them you were probably just in drag, says Fern.

You're fucking right, I say, smiling at the men.

One of the guys shrugs, sipping his drink. The other man squints at me, mumbling under his breath—but I'm already gone.

It isn't long before the room starts thinning out.

Which happens gradually. And then instantly. Which is the kind of night that we can't afford, whether Fern admits it or not—so maybe that's why, all of a sudden, the bar door opens with a clatter and our landlord steps in, slick in a coat and boots and setting up at the counter.

I've never actually met Cecilia. I've only heard about her in bits and pieces. Whenever her name pops up, Fern's nothing but adulatory, and Minh only makes the same pained frown. In our little world, she's a fucking VIP.

So I slide her a Coke.

I ask how she's doing.

Delightful, says Cecilia.

It's been a pretty busy night, I say.

Less so with every second that passes, says Cecilia.

We do what we can, I say. It seems to be hard all over the neighborhood.

That's enough for Cecilia to look up from her phone. She considers me, smiling.

Where are you from, she asks.

Here, I say.

That means nothing in Houston.

So I tell her about Galveston and she smiles.

My family lived by the coast for a time, she says. They're scattered between here and Oaxaca. But they always liked Galveston best.

Yeah?

Yes. Thrilling place to raise a family. Are your parents still there?

I have family there, I say, but I don't feel the need to elaborate.

And what brought you to Harry's, says Cecilia.

Circumstance, I say.

Is that right?

I needed a change of pace, I say—another half-truth.

You've picked an interesting time to drop in, she says. Montrose is changing. For the longest time, these bars used to be the only place for queer people in Houston to go. But now we've all got the internet. It's easier to order in.

I think Harry's is worth it, I say.

Me too, says Cecilia. And that's why I pay your salary. Are you going to offer me a real drink?

Before I can open my mouth, Minh's beside me, mixing her a sex on the beach.

Thanks, dear, says Cecilia.

Always, says Minh.

He delivers it without any snark. It's the nicest I've ever seen him.

And just like that, Fern appears, too, smiling as wide as his face will allow. As he takes Cecilia's hand, Minh and I watch them head toward the staff room.

Pack up when it makes sense, Fern calls out.

Sí, capitán, we yell.

An hour later, we're empty.

Minh and I Swiffer from end to end of the bar. Once we've hit a stopping point, he reaches behind the counter, feeling around his fanny pack for a wad of aluminum foil.

Try this, he says, handing me some meat wrapped in rice paper. I take one roll, before he hands me another, and the two of us settle against the wall.

This is fucking delicious, I say.

It's nem nướng, says Minh. And that's the most I've seen you eat since you got hired.

Shut up, I say.

You shut up. I've been trying to get a fatter ass.

Is that your latest goal?

It's up there.

Then I think you're well on your way.

We're all works in progress, says Minh. How'd it go with Cecilia?

She seems nice enough.

That's a stretch, says Minh. But she's fair, which is better. And she's Fern's cousin or something. The building's in her name.

If they're family, then why's he pressed?

He's pressed *because* she's family, says Minh. Even with the deals she's scoring for him, we're barely clearing enough every month. If our lease ended tomorrow, she could probably double the rent.

Minh and I let that number hang in the air.

And it absolutely makes sense.

So who's that guy again, says Minh. The one you keep hovering around.

I told you, I say.

Probably wasn't listening.

A childhood friend.

Weird, says Minh. And here I was thinking you arrived from the ether.

I don't know, I say. It's weird seeing people I knew from before Kai died.

For a second, I expect Minh to say I'm killing the mood.

Or that I need to calm down.

Or that the point I'm making isn't a point at all, just a fucking excuse.

But he doesn't do any of that.

He shrugs.

Haven't seen the friend around lately, says Minh. He was cute.

You're not his type, I say.

What does that even mean?

He only goes for lost causes.

Don't we all, says Minh. Did you scare him off?

Maybe, I say. But I didn't mean to.

Then tell him that.

Nah. It's complicated.

So uncomplicate it, says Minh.

He laughs, handing me another wrap.

This time, I take it immediately. It's still just as delicious.

There's this dream I keep having.

Kai and I are drinking on our balcony. We're three years in. He's cooking dinner for once, because he's finally finished a months-long translation project, and it's a slab of salmon marinated in miso. I tell him to keep an eye on the stove, and Kai tells me to relax, and it's a window of dickishness from him but I don't say anything about it. I pop a Xanax instead.

I offer Kai one, too.

He blinks a few times before he downs it.

It's cool outside. One of the rare August nights in LA when the breeze flits in, just a little bit, and you feel this chill along your spine and all through your home—so we say fuck it and sit on our balcony, with the stove still fuming, and the two of us laugh over the thought of two southern queers sitting on a California windowsill stoned out of their heads, and what do you call that, Kai spurts, birds on a fucking stoop?

For some reason, that's hilarious. We laugh so hard that we're rocking in our chairs, and we can hardly catch our balance or our breath, and Kai tells me to be careful from his corner, standing and steadying himself on the railing, but he doesn't actually catch himself so he misses the bar and he falls, and I watch him sink, and I can't tell you why but my eyes shut before he hits the ground, maybe my body simply *knew*, it must have decided to shut itself off, and I turn from where Kai was just sitting back to where he's ended up, and when the scream leaves my body the stove's timer sounds off, too—we're both yelling about the same thing, we both need to be attended to.

Don't fucking lie, says Kai.

It's not a lie, I say.

But it isn't what happened, says Kai.

Tonight, he's snickering, sitting cross-legged on my bed in Fern's house. I woke up from his death to find him cackling across from me, sporting go-go boy shorts and a spandex harness.

It could've, I say.

But it didn't, says Kai. And you're saying it's my fault?

Nobody's death is anyone's fault. Everyone dies.

You don't really believe that.

Shut up, I say. Shut up, shut up, shut up.

Tough guy. Yelling at a ghost.

I'm serious.

And so am I, Kai says.

No, I say. You're nothing. This is nothing. You're fucking dead.

We wouldn't be here if you really believed that, says Kai.

That weekend, I finally give in: the bakery hasn't changed.

It's really just a house in the Heights. The property sits on a tidy block bundled by bungalows, flanked by a dive bar and a loan shark and some crumbling one-story apartments. There's a Lao restaurant and a florist and a McDonald's. The street's tapered off by a bail-bonds shop. Turn west, and you'll hit a row of glossy boutiques. Flip east, and the houses turn modest, mostly worn down and colorful. There's a Mexican church that's loomed over the block since forever. An assortment of cantinas and markets and daycares fill out the boulevards behind it.

But most of the homes I walked by as a kid are long gone. My old place, too. They've all been flipped into BnBs. There's a tiny church with a pride flag. And then there's a glitzy barbershop. A row of glass-covered craft shops.

The bakery looks the same though.

Almost too fucking familiar.

I almost turn right the fuck around, but I pop a Valium in the parking lot and that's enough to get me inside.

The window is stuffed with sweets. Oatmeal cookies and multicolor macarons and red bean buns and almond bear claws and strawberry galettes and mini walnut tarts and butter mochi balls and chocolate muffins and kimchi-cheddar scones and vanilla blondies and loaf after loaf of milk bread. Behind the register, a lady with tattoos lining her arms taps away at a tablet. Beside her, an older guy drips coffee into the carafe, singing amor de something in Spanish.

He smiles when he turns my way, like we're both in on the same fucking joke. But the woman just stares me down.

Hey, I say, is Mae here?

Neither of them says anything.

The lady leans across the counter, revealing even more tattoos.

Are you a friend, she asks.

Kind of, I say. Are you?

Comparatively. Because you don't seem very friendly.

I know this house a lot better than you do.

And yet here you are, says this lady. Looking lost.

She should be back soon, says the man, smiling again.

He steps forward now, offering a hand. I bump his fist instead.

I'm Ivan, he says. She's Fati. Are you here about the property?

No, I say.

Then what do you need, says Fati.

I used to live here, I say.

Ivan and Fati turn to each other. Then Fati slaps a towel on the counter, turning up the hall, toward the rest of the house.

So you're TJ's friend, says Ivan.

Yes and no, I say. Have you been here long?

I've worked with Mae for a few years now.

With or for?

Ivan smiles at this, sipping his coffee.

Mae's great, he says.

And TJ, I ask.

Her son is a lovely young man, says Ivan, smiling even wider.

It sounds like bullshit. But Ivan doesn't seem like a bullshitter. And before I can say anything else, the door slams open behind him—and Fati is followed by TJ, glaring under his cap. He's got flour all over his apron, shuffling in some Crocs.

What the *fuck* are you doing here, he says.

Calm down, I say.

No, says TJ. You have no—

You said you wanted to see me. That I should come visit Mae. Here I am.

I fucking told you to *text* me.

So I cut out the middleman, I say.

This is what you *always* fucking do, says TJ. It's too fucking *much*.

You've really cleaned up the place, I say.

Maybe you two should go in the back, says Fati.

She gives TJ an annoyed look, not even glancing my way. But she isn't wrong. A line of customers has formed behind me, trickling through the door. Some Black high schoolers. A huddle of white women.

When I turn to TJ, he's still huffing and puffing. But he nods at the stairwell behind him.

Upstairs, I sit on the floor while TJ flops across the sofa. It's a tiny game room, but we arrange ourselves until we're hardly in danger of touching. The house cat, Mochi, unfurls himself from a corner, brushing my leg on his way down the hallway.

TJ crosses his legs, tapping at his phone, while I take in the surroundings.

It's uncanny how little has changed.

It makes me fucking nauseous.

Even the couch, I say.

What, says TJ.

Nothing, I say. It all just feels the same.

Mae insists on it, says TJ.

The same way you insist on calling your mom by her first name.

How the fuck would I look calling her *Mom* at work?

Like her son, I say.

Well, says TJ, but he doesn't say anything else.

Downstairs, we hear Ivan laughing, and Fati cussing him out. The entry bell dings at a steady pace.

Remember how we said we'd both get out of here, I say.

TJ stops tapping at his phone. But he doesn't look up.

You sound like a fucking whitegirl, says TJ.

I'm serious, I say.

Sure, Ladybird. That leaving shit was more *you* than me.

It was too claustrophobic. Things just got easier outside of Texas.

I'm happy you feel that way, says TJ.

There's a question that I play a few times in my head before it leaves my mouth.

Why did you come to the bar, I ask. And don't lie this time.

With that, TJ finally looks up at me. He sets his phone in his lap, crossing his arms. He's wearing tracksuit bottoms, and the fabric hugs his thighs.

I was in the area, he says. That's it.

Really?

Really. I didn't plan on saying shit to you.

But you did say something.

Yeah, says TJ. Lucky me.

So you knew I'd be there, I say, and TJ just snorts.

The two of us sit silently.

TJ wipes his hands on his sweats.

But I've been worried about you, says TJ. Obviously. After what happened. So, yes, I have been wondering how you were doing, and now I know. You seem fine.

Thanks for your approval, I say.

But it's not like you called me when you came back either, says TJ. That was a choice, too.

You can't be serious, I say.

Never mind, says TJ.

No. Say what you need to say.

I have shit to do, says TJ.

He stands, reaching for his apron. As he guides it over his neck, a cloud of flour floats around him.

It's already the afternoon, I say.

And?

Jin only worked until midday.

Mae runs a tighter ship, says TJ.

Okay, I say. But tell me something. Are you out now?

That's enough to make TJ blush. He spins around, clearly fuming.

I was never *not* out, he says.

Right, I say. Discreet. Whatever.

Everyone doesn't fucking have to be like you!

But I never thought I'd see you at a gay bar, I say.

Before I can finish my sentence, I hear steps behind me. TJ raises a palm to shut me up, which is when Mae sets a hand on my shoulder.

She's a little shorter than me. There's a bit of gray sprinkled in her hair, but her skin is radiant. And her smile's still warm. Like it hasn't been over a decade.

Great talk, says TJ.

He brushes past me and his mother, stomping back downstairs.

I turn to see him go, and then I look down at Mae.

Hey, stranger, she says.

Hey, I say.

You could've called, she says, and I nod, although I'm not sure whether she's talking about today specifically or all of the other times.

Mae still takes hold of my palm, feeling the center. She squeezes my fingertips.

She tells me I should stay for dinner.

I can't, I say. But I'll come back.

Is that right, says Mae. Like you came back last time?

We've made it downstairs, standing out on the driveway. The road behind us sits empty. The high school's classes are already finished but it's too early for the assortment of day workers and spinsters and drunks who bumble around the Heights. When we were kids, TJ and I sat on the same concrete, baking under the sun, until his father stepped out of the house with rice drinks and pastries. He'd share them with us, rustling our hair while we watched the passersby.

But now the road's a few years out from being crowded by a bunch of fucking sports bars.

And a CrossFit gym.

And some tidy white-owned businesses.

Mae catches me looking around. She hooks her arm through my elbow.

Call *me* next time, says Mae. And don't stay away so long. Everything won't feel like it's changed so much.

It's just shocking.

A little. But everything changes, and we're still here. Are you really doing all right?

Nothing to report.

You're okay for money?

I'm fine.

TJ said you're working at a bar now?

Something like that.

And you're on a diet? You're looking pretty light, hon.

My weight's just fluctuating. That happens.

It does, says Mae. But this is quite a fluctuation.

It's fine, I say. I'm fine.

Loquacious as ever, says Mae. You're always welcome back here. You know what Jin said.

I remember, I say.

Good, says Mae.

I pull up the rideshare app on my phone. The next free car's only a few blocks away. But before I step off, I turn back to Mae.

Hey, I say. I'm sorry I never visited after Jin died. That was wrong.

Which makes Mae smile again.

But this one's different.

Weary.

It wasn't wrong, she says. It just *is*.

Get home safe, she adds, and I tell her that I'll try.

The driver's a hefty brown guy in his thirties. He tells me that he's just moved to Alief. And he's in a neck brace, so when I ask him what happened, he laughs and calls it a basketball accident: he leapt when he should've dipped. We're silent most of the ride.

When we stop at a light on Studemont, an idea starts to form. I don't know where it comes from. But I reach forward and put my hand on the driver's waist. And he keeps driving, not turning my way as I reach into his shorts, and I can feel that he's stiffened.

He grunts when he comes.

I wipe the mess on the inside of his leg.

Once we've parked, I tell him I hope he feels better soon, and he laughs, waving, thanking me.

Another thing Kai liked to say: love is a tangible thing.

It is palpable.

You can hold it in your hands.

You can see it in the air.

You can breathe it in and hold it and push that shit right back out of your lungs. When it dissolves, you might not see it, but that won't mean it wasn't there.

Because *you* were.

Kai and I rarely fought but there were fights.

Our central argument never changed: he swore I wasn't as committed. He was invested and I wasn't.

You can't say that, I'd tell him. You can't know what anyone else is thinking.

I don't have to, said Kai. It's in your *actions*. It's the way you fucking *move*.

One night early on, at some bar in WeHo, Kai told a guy I was dancing with to fuck off. He'd stepped away to grab us drinks. Another dude took his place. It wasn't anything serious, but Kai called the man a bitch and a cousinfucker and a slut, and when that guy finally pissed off, Kai laced his arms through my elbows. We continued dancing, and then we left the bar, and we never actually talked about it but I started being more careful.

We'd run through our histories early on. This was a quick conversation. Kai told me that he'd been around, and I believed him. He said he didn't need to know who I'd fucked before him. But one week, when we were still open, I came down with chlamydia, and gonorrhea, and because my luck is my luck my herpes broke out, too, and when I told Kai this had happened he made a serious face, like he was about to fucking explode. We were lounging in sweats at his place. I'd stressed all day about how to tell him. But all Kai did was burst into laughter over his cup ramen. For weeks and weeks afterward, he'd joke about how nervous I looked. It wasn't much longer before he asked if I wanted to try being exclusive, at least for a little while. At the very least, he told me I'd probably save cash on trips to the clinic.

One week, Kai flew back home to see his sister. It had something to do with his mother. They weren't very close. But he still flew overnight from Osaka, where he was working, to Baton Rouge, and when he made it back to LA, Kai told me he wouldn't be seeing his family again.

We were in an Ethiopian restaurant when he said it. Sitting outdoors, pushing around the rice in front of us.

Why not, I said.

Don't get me started, said Kai.

But they want to see you, I said. And everybody doesn't have that.

You don't know what you're talking about, said Kai.

I know better than most, I said. You're lucky your family's still here. You'll hate yourself for the rest of your life if you let them go.

Kai's eyes flared up then. Which had never happened before. He was usually cool, usually calm.

A server approached our table, but then he saw Kai's face and thought better of it.

Let's stick with what we know, said Kai, and you don't know shit about my people.

I know that they're *there*, I said.

You know what I've *told* you.

Do you have any idea what I'd do to see my fucking parents again, I said.

But that's *you,* said Kai. That's *your* life.

So tell me what's going on with your family!

Kai prodded the injera in front of him, dragging everything through his sauce. And another, braver, waitress dropped by our table. She asked gently if we needed any water, or if we were done with our meal, and I looked up to see the entire restaurant staring our way.

We didn't speak on our walk back to his place. But eventually, Kai nodded toward the park, asking if I wanted to take a detour. He was always doing this, floating around finding little patches of green. Kai pointed up at the jacarandas and I told him they were beautiful.

When we made it back to his place, he put his mouth on mine. The sex began as a routine exercise, but it quickly became something else. His body felt like a new, visceral thing. I guess mine did, too. And Kai was fucking me, so I told him to go faster, and when his pace quickened I told him to fuck me harder. When he began again, groaning, I hit his shoulders, and he met my eyes, and he hit a new wind but there was a force that wasn't present before.

After Kai collapsed on top of me, I squeezed him. We didn't leap toward the bathroom. We just lay with our legs wrapped around each other.

I apologized.

He told me it was fine.

I told Kai that I'd stay, and that I needed him to stay.

Kai told me he was one and done, and I said that wasn't what I meant.

Then he just blinked.

And Kai said, Okay.

Kai liked saying that people couldn't recognize a good thing if it hit them square in the fucking face.

But we're different, I said. Me and you.

And Kai only smiled.

He never flew back home again. Every few months, when he'd normally go back to Louisiana for a visit, Kai simply told his sister that something had come up.

When Kai comes to me now, all he does is laugh. A malicious cackle. Something he never did in life.

When I'm showering, he grins with his legs crossed on the toilet.

When I'm cooking at night after work, he floats through the kitchen, yawning beside me.

When I'm walking down the street, Kai burps a few steps behind me, with his hands on his head, whistling whole symphonies into my ear.

Sometimes, I wonder about what I'll say when he shows up. I list the topics in my head. Stack them from most to least important. And then, all of a sudden, Kai's right in my face, clicking his tongue against the edge of my eardrum, until whatever I have for him is gone.

One day, while I'm cooking breakfast for Jake and Fern, Kai flicks the back of my neck.

I almost reach out to grab him before I catch myself.

There's no reason for this, I whisper. You weren't like this.

Bullshit, says Kai. You mean that this isn't how you *remember* me.

It isn't how you left me. This wasn't you.

Don't beg and then try to choose, says Kai.

My new life in Houston, or whatever the fuck you'd call it, has condensed itself into something like a routine.

I work at Harry's, taking shots with Minh behind the counter.

I walk Diego to school.

I cook for Fern and Jake on my days off, then we watch shitty movies until we all start snoring.

It's the most comfortable I've been in months.

But it doesn't feel sustainable.

Something always feels off.

And then there's the fucking.

It's a little like magic: I'll think of a man, and all of a sudden he's there. It's always someone from an app. Or the internet. Or some guy loitering around the back of Harry's a little too long, dropping a pin or a DM or staring me right in the face.

Sometimes it's the exact sort of guy that I'm looking for: lanky, chubby, short, tall, hairy, smooth, softer, sharper, bald, older, straight-ish, queeny, whatever. And sometimes it isn't. But I find a way to make it work, because that's just the way it fucking goes. Sometimes he's got weed and sometimes he's got K and sometimes he's got G and it feels like a miracle every time.

One time, I fuck a guy on the bathroom floor in Kroger while his wife shops for crawfish, haggling with the cashier while I stretch her husband out.

One time, I fuck a man the night before his wedding. I know this because he pops up on my app downtown, not too far from his hotel. When I meet him, he's waving goodbye to some bachelor party buddies, and he asks if I'm clean, and he asks again an hour later, except I'm already fucking him and we're already high and he yells for me not to pull out.

One time—many times—I fuck whoever's cruising the bars while I'm on break: he'll sit on the patio of the diner across from our emergency exit, tapping at his phone, pretending to wait for his friends, and we'll end up sticking our hands in each other's pants.

One time, I'm at the Home Depot picking up some paint for Fern, because Jake insists that he doesn't have the time, and an employee follows me into the bathroom, standing beside me at the urinal, and he starts stroking himself, so I follow suit, and we both finish facing the wall, holding our breath, and this guy goes back to work and I finally find the paint but he's the one who ends up checking me out for the purchase.

One time, I get a message from a Black woman who wants me to fuck her husband, and when I pull up to their place they meet me at the door. The guy shakes my hand. His wife offers me a beer. When I say I'm actually not drinking, they bring out a baggie of coke instead. It's a perfectly vanilla evening until the wife leaves the room, because that's when the husband gets nervous, sweating, swearing that he doesn't know what's supposed to happen now, so I take the lead, and by the time I'm inside him his wife's kicked back in a chair across from us, sipping a glass of wine.

One time, in the middle of the day, I get a ping from somebody's condo in East Montrose, and when I finally get there I see at least five different cars in the parking lot, and then nine different guys in the living room, although I can't really tell with the lights out, but the feel of their faces and arms and cocks are entirely different, and I couldn't tell you who did what, but I recall the sounds we made, and the way that we blended together until we were all one sound. And I take a tab of their Molly, and I take a hit of their T, and that's when all of the room's colors fold into themselves, inside me, and there's a knock at the door, and the house's owner—a whiteguy, obviously—opens it to find a chubby Latino repair dude squinting into the living room, asking about fixing the fan, but we invite him in and he doesn't say no and eventually he becomes a part of the void, too.

One time, I meet a Chinese guy at his college. He's just graduated. The ceremony's over and he's still in his suit—the cap and gown and everything. He says the one thing he'd wanted to accomplish before his visa expired was sex with a man, and I laugh, and when he asks why I tell him that this is hardly an accomplishment. It's a thing that he can do at any hour of any day of any calendar year. But this guy kisses me before I can leave, so I unbutton his shirt, and then his slacks, and we both stand in our boxers while he shivers, and he tells me he's been rehearsing this moment in his head for years, and this isn't how he saw it happening at all.

And that was funny.

Like, I laugh out loud.

I tell him, That's life, and I'm already zonked, so I fuck him for six hours.

The third time he comes, he's got tears in his eyes, and when I ask him what's wrong he just says that he's happy.

Fucking ridiculous, says Kai.

You and I weren't exactly chaste, I say.

This is different, says Kai. There's a cost.

But you aren't here to stop me, I say.

One morning, I'm walking Diego to school and he's clunking his sneakers against the concrete. It's a new thing. Lately, he's only gotten more and more sullen. The kid's gone from practically levitating over breakfast to glowering nearly all the time. Jake says it's Fern's fault. Fern blames his ex. And his ex, according to Fern, simply chalks it up to Diego's age.

But now Diego's knocking his violin case along the curb. When he hits it a third time, the case nearly catapults open.

Hey man, I say, you're gonna hurt yourself.

I'm fine, says Diego.

Did something happen?

No.

Are you being bullied? Do I need to kick someone's father?

No.

Are you mad about something? Are you mad at me?

Do you think the whole fucking world revolves around you?

Don't say fuck.

You say it all the *time*.

But not to you. And I'm only asking questions.

Then don't ask, says Diego. And it's not your fault. I'm just having a bad week.

That is definitely a thing that happens, I say. Is it because of anything in particular?

Yeah. People.

Okay. That's a start.

Dumb people.

Closer, I say. Are we talking about friends? Or not-friends?

Not-friends, says Diego. Bullies. But not really.

Okay. Why not really?

Because it's not like they're beating me up. They're not really calling me names. But they just, you know, talk about my dads. And they talk shit about me. Only not around me. But, sometimes, right in front of me. It doesn't happen a lot.

Like homophobic things?

Not really. Or not always. Sometimes they'll call me fat. Or dirty.

Diego, I say. Fucking hell. How long has this been happening?

I don't know. A little while.

Like a few weeks?

I guess. Maybe longer.

Okay, I say. Thanks for telling me, Diego. I'm sorry you're dealing with that. What would you like me to do?

God, says Diego. This is why I didn't want to tell you!

You don't have to deal with things like that, I say. Nobody should. You don't have to just ignore it. Have you told anybody?

I told my mom.

And what did she say?

She wanted to call the school, but I asked her not to. So she said to tell my dad.

I'll talk to him, I say, and Diego immediately throws me a glare.

No, he says, I don't want *you* to *do* anything. And it's not like I live at school. I just have to get through this year.

Diego.

Cam.

The kid looks up at me. We pause beside the curb, just under a cluster of heavy tree branches.

Is it okay if we just walk without talking, says Diego.

Always, I say.

And we keep strolling.

But Diego doesn't look at me. He just keeps clunking. And then, scraping over a curb, the heel of his sneaker catches, and when he jerks his foot, the sole separates itself entirely. The kid only just barely manages to catch himself before the rest of his shoe falls apart.

When I turn to Diego, he looks distraught. We're about a block from his school.

Look, I say. Don't worry about it. I'll grab another pair and bring it to you now.

I'm sorry, says Diego. I'm sorry! I didn't—

It's fine.

But I didn't—

It's *fine*, I say. Really. Just go to class and I'll swing by later.

Jogging toward the building with the half-broken shoe, Diego gives me a long look before he sighs.

Then he smirks.

Thanks, Cam, he says.

It's nothing, I say, and I wait until he's gone before I start heading back.

That night, I make it back to Fern's place after closing up the bar and he's already dozing on the sofa beside Jake. They're lounging in matching hoodies, watching a muted *Lord of the Rings*. If they were white, then they might have been a stock queer couple's photo. But Jake looks up when I close the door, waving.

Come watch Sam kill this tarantula, he says.

I have no fucking idea what that means, I say.

You only need to see the last hour. I'll fill in the blanks.

So I sit on the floor in between them. Fern snorts, and I think he's awake. But he falls back asleep just as suddenly.

I thought Diego was staying over tonight, I say.

His mom said something came up, says Jake. A school thing. He'll be here tomorrow morning.

Isn't that what happened last time?

It's what happens every time, says Jake. Look, this part's important.

We watch a pair of little dudes run headfirst into a set of gates. It's obvious that they don't stand much of a chance, at least to me. But they keep running anyway. And Jake's totally absorbed.

A scream rips through the apartment window, breaking the film's trance. Jake and I turn to each other. But the screech is followed by a woman's laughter and the honking of some car horns on Fairview.

I ask Jake if he's hungry for anything.

There's takeout on the counter, he says.

From around here? Was it any good?

Jake purses his lips into a not-smile. It's a regular in his repertoire.

So I stand, heading into the kitchen, and Jake doesn't stop me. When I make it back out, I hand him a lopsided omelet, covered in bean sprouts and cilantro and chili garlic sauce, squeezing half a lime across its edges.

Jesus, he says.

Nope, just me, I say.

Where's yours?

I ate at the bar.

Still, says Jake, and he slices his omelet in half, reaching across the coffee table for a packaged set of silverware.

So I take one bite.

And then another.

I manage to get it down.

When I grin at Jake, he's cheesing, and we both turn back to the screen.

You know, says Jake, I was pretty pissed when Fern suggested that you live with us. It felt unfair.

I always thought the two of you had talked it out.

Sure. But I meant unfair to *you*. I didn't know much yet, but I knew you were grieving. It seemed wrong to put you in a new city. In a house with strangers.

You're not too strange, I say.

You haven't met my family, says Jake.

Can't be that bad if they ended up with you, I say.

The words pop out a little too quickly.

Jake makes a funny face.

But before I can deflect, he puts a finger over his lips, pointing at the screen.

The hobbits have managed to squeeze through the gates after all. They huddle together, shielding each other from the fire and lava spewing toward them.

Are they queer, I ask.

Nah, says Jake.

Too bad. It'd make a better movie.

We can't have everything, says Jake, laughing.

Some nights, Kai's deaths in my dreams are worse than others.

He falls down an elevator shaft at the bank. He trips in the apartment and knocks his head on the counter. He chokes on a fish bone, grasping at the table. He falls asleep under anesthesia and never wakes up. He overdoses on pills. He overdoses on a needle. He hangs himself. He simply collapses onto the sidewalk.

But then, in these dreams, Kai always opens his eyes.

Brushes himself off.

He comes back to me, laughing.

Easier to spend time dwelling on death than it is to live, says Kai.

How could you fucking say that, I say.

Because it's true.

Did you die and become a fucking monk? Did we live in the same world? How the fuck can you know what you know and still say that?

I didn't say it was easy, says Kai. Just easier.

The beginning of yet another end of my world starts with an argument.

Or the lack thereof.

Cecilia's raising our rent.

Fern tells me and Jake over dinner. It's raining for the first time in weeks. I've cooked boxed Japanese curry for the three of us, with some shrimp and squash and nuts stirred into the roux. So we're well into the meal when Fern says it, casually throwing out the number.

It's another few seconds before the digits register. Jake nearly spits out his prawns.

Sixty-five *hundred* dollars, says Jake. Is that what you just said?

They're Cecilia's terms, says Fern.

Fernando, says Jake. Do you hear yourself?

It's something we'll work through. A tiny problem.

No, says Jake. That is the fucking apocalypse.

This wasn't entirely inaccurate. The money question is sensitive between Fern and Jake. It's the only time I ever see them argue, but these discussions are always showstoppers. They yell. Throw shit. Flick lights on and off. Usually, Fern has some sort of retort for all of it: We'll earn the cash through an event. The next month will be busier.

But now he just eats silently. Chewing away at his curry.

You said you had the revenue, says Jake. You said this wouldn't be a fucking problem.

When did I say that, says Fern. When did you hear that come out of my mouth?

Not even a week ago!

Bueno, pero Cecilia switched up on me. What's good for her isn't necessarily good for us.

You *refuse* to do what's good for us. What would be *good* for us is fucking selling the bar.

That's not an option, says Fern.

And Cecilia's actually been generous, adds Fern. Every other place in Montrose has priced up. I tried asking Cristina for help, but—

Wait, says Jake, when did you do that? Why the fuck would you do that?

Does it matter?

Yes. It fucking matters to me that you're asking your *ex-wife* for *cash*. You said you wanted to own a business, but you don't even know what that looks like.

What the fuck are you even talking about?

If you spent as much time worrying about your *ex* as you do this dumbass dead-end *bar*—

All I'm saying is that she offered to help!

If she helped any more then she'd own the fucking place herself, says Jake, and the look Fern gives him is one I didn't even know he could make.

Their voices turn hoarse. Then Jake looks like he's checked out. He turns to me, just for a second, but I don't say shit, because I know there's nothing to say. It's the face of inevitability. I recognize it immediately because I've worn it so often myself.

TJ says I'm biting off more than I can chew. It's the weekend, and we're drinking on the patio of an East End hipster haunt. Everyone else is white, and probably straight, but the crowd's still lively, all beers and laughs and yelling in each other's faces about the Texans.

When I ask TJ about the last time he's been to a straight bar, he makes a face, blowing a plume of weed at my nose.

Don't be stupid, he says.

Didn't you only come out like two minutes ago?

I was never—

Okay.

And it doesn't matter, says TJ. You just like complaining about queers who aren't like you.

Did I say that?

No. You were too busy boning everything in sight.

And *you* live like you have something to hide, I say. What I'm doing doesn't hurt anyone. Kai's fucking gone.

And this is how you deal with that?

I don't think you get to talk to me about who I sleep with.

I watch TJ open his mouth, but then he closes it. He takes a sip of his water instead.

Whatever, he says. I haven't seen Ian in weeks.

That's a name I haven't heard in a while, I say.

You haven't heard it because you haven't asked.

I haven't asked because it gives me heartburn.

We watch a one-eared pit bull eye us from across the road, lazing on the ground off-leash. There's no owner around. With every wasted patron that passes, the dog raises his eyes, sighing.

Isn't he married, I ask.

That hasn't happened yet, says TJ.

Yet, I say. Great. That's sensational. I don't know what you even see in—

You don't have to, says TJ. You're not fucking him.

Thank god.

And it isn't your business anyways.

If you say so, I say. I just think you—

Stop, says TJ. Can't you just let this be?

A pair of whiteboys throw a hot dog bun toward the pit bull. But the dog only stares at it tentatively, shaking his head.

Eventually, he rolls on his side, exasperated.

I just don't want to see you get hurt, I say. That's all.

That's new for you, says TJ.

Fine. Be a dickhead.

I tell TJ that I'm taking a piss, and he asks me to grab another water on the way back. But I end up standing beside a whiteboy outside the restroom.

He smiles. I smile.

We both look at our feet, tapping them to the punk playing above us.

When the door opens, a whitelady yelps at the sight of me, apologizing immediately. Then the whiteboy laughs. And I do, too. As he steps inside the bathroom, he doesn't close the door behind him.

We don't take too long.

Afterward, I bring TJ his water.

He squints at me.

Did you actually want Topo Chico, I ask.

No, says TJ.

Then what?

Don't worry about it.

Say what you need to say.

I don't know, says TJ. I just worry about you.

He looks genuinely concerned, scratching his forehead. I reach for his vape pen, blowing a little pot in the air.

Thanks, I say, but I'm very grown.

That's the problem, says TJ.

It's been so long since we've gone out together that I've forgotten our rhythm. The next place we drive to is well across the city: a tiny Korean restaurant in Spring, nestled between row upon row of loan sharks, churches, and pawn-shops.

I recognize the place eventually. TJ's father brought us here whenever Mae was out of town. He'd greet the owners in Korean, chatting with the couple while TJ and I kicked each other under the table. After Jin died, I never came back.

The tables are glossy, just like I remember. No menus in sight. Everything's separated by glass partitions, topped with plastic water jugs. Kim Jung Mi tin-kles from the speakers above us, and the waitress, probably a high schooler, hands us cups and lists off the specials.

TJ starts speaking in English, before he switches to Korean, and the waitress cocks her head but she doesn't miss a beat. She repeats the order, and TJ nods, smiling for the first time all evening. It disappears as soon as she's gone.

You're getting seolleongtang, says TJ.

Thanks, Dad, I say. I always forget you speak Korean.

I'm going to pretend you didn't say that, he says.

You hated practicing with Jin.

That was years ago, says TJ. Mae needed someone to talk to our old distributors.

I thought she was fluent, too?

She nearly is, says TJ. But I'm the son.

That's gross, I say, and TJ just shrugs.

When the server returns, she's got two bowls of soup, and some rice, and also stewed potatoes, a seaweed salad, some cold macaroni, pickled radish, kimchi, salted cucumbers, and a platter of braised fish. I ask for a beer, and she gives me a funny look, but then TJ adds something in Korean and she laughs him off.

Once she's gone, TJ says, I told her you were kidding.

That's funny because I wasn't.

The owners died in a drunk-driving accident. They stopped selling alcohol here afterward.

Fuck. I didn't know.

How would you, says TJ. It'd require you to care about someone else.

The broth is hot. A crowded table of business dudes guffaws in the booth beside us. Behind them, a mother and her son chip away at a bowl of glass noodles. And three women gasp over a hot plate, while one shakes her head and the others repeat, You don't fucking *need* that, I would've fucking *killed* him.

When I look up again, TJ's staring.

You're not gonna eat anything else, he asks.

I'm getting to it, I say.

You didn't have anything at the bar either.

Is that a problem? Are you the CIA?

No. I just—

Maybe you eat too fucking much. Did you ever think about that?

Nice, says TJ.

Hey, I say. Wait. I didn't mean—

It's fine, he says.

At the table behind us, the woman sitting with her son catches my eye. I nod at her. She grins back, snorting.

What did you and Kai eat in LA, says TJ.

We don't have to talk about him, I say.

You didn't put a gun to my head. I'm asking because I want to know.

TJ sets his spoon down, cracking his knuckles.

A lot of Mexican food, I say. And Japanese, obviously.

For work?

Yeah. Sometimes he made simple stuff for his job. And he baked.

For real?

Yeah. There was this pudding his mother made. That was his weekend thing.

How was it?

Pretty good.

Did you ever bake for him, asks TJ.

Sure, I say. He has a sweet tooth.

I don't realize what I've said until a moment later.

TJ doesn't correct me. He's already chewing again.

When our waitress returns, she asks how I'm doing. I tell her I'm fine, and TJ asks for the bill—but that's when some guy appears at our table out of nowhere.

He's short. Scruffy. Beaming when he speaks. It's enough for TJ to stop chewing, and this guy wrings his hands, asking if TJ's been to the restaurant before.

All the time, says TJ.

Even when you were younger, asks this guy.

Yeah, says TJ, turning to me.

I just blink back at him. And the guy claps, cheesing from ear to ear.

Then you're Jin's son, he says, extending his hand—apparently, he's the child of the owners. He'd been living out in Dallas. Took over the restaurant a few months ago.

TJ turns a deep amber.

It's been years since I've seen him blush.

Jonah, says TJ.

You remembered!

Of course.

I always wondered how you were doing, says Jonah.

We were babies, says TJ.

Yeah. Well. We're here now.

I look at TJ.

TJ looks at Jonah.

Then Jonah smiles at me.

So I tell TJ that I'll wait outside. Before he can cobble an excuse together, I stand, setting a hand on his shoulder.

Shuffling by the car, I feel around in my pocket for an Adderall, and I've just managed to down it before TJ finally joins me.

He's still shaking his head. Still blushing.

Jonah's cute, I say.

He was just saying hi, says TJ.

No one just says *hi*.

Shut up.

You'd make a handsome couple.

I'd rather be cute.

We can't all get what we want, I say. But I'm happy for you. Wait until he finds out about your head game.

Shut *up*, says TJ. He's not even gay.

Right. And I'm a fucking pastor.

It was nothing, says TJ, unlocking his car, but he only sounds warmer the second time.

. . .

At some point, I realize we're taking the long way home. We drive through Memorial, until we hit Westheimer, winding northward as Montrose melts into Studemont. We're only a few blocks from the house when TJ pulls into this park beside the feeder road.

Once he's settled the car, he just sits there. Staring through the window. It's a moment that feels pregnant with another moment, but I'm not sure what the next step is. It's been too long between us.

Are we about to kiss, I say.

Fuck you, says TJ, rubbing his eyes.

Outside our window, some kids tiptoe across a tightrope on the playground. They're singing a song in Mandarin, but I can hardly make out the words.

Look, says TJ. I know we haven't talked in a while—

We've been talking all night, I say.

You know that's not what I mean, says TJ. I just, honestly, want to know if you're okay.

Do I not look okay to you?

TJ turns to the windshield. He bites his bottom lip.

I think something is going on with you and food and maybe other stuff, he says, and when he turns to look my way, I don't say anything to that.

I think you should talk to someone, says TJ. And it doesn't have to be me. But I think you should reach out to a professional, like a therapist, maybe. And I can help you with that, if you want. And I won't even pretend to understand what you're dealing with, because there's no way I could. That just wouldn't be possible. And I can't imagine the burden of it all. But I think you're still trying to deal. And I think what you're going through is really, really hard. And I just think, you know, it might help to find resources for navigating it? Something to help you?

Okay, I say.

The word feels like a hook in my throat. I have to cough it out. And I feel fucking nauseous.

Thanks for your concern, I say. Truly.

I'm saying that you can talk to me, says TJ. And that we don't have to say everything at once. I can just shut up and listen, if that's what you want. It's fucking hard to do this shit alone, and you don't have to do that, and I don't want to see you get hurt. I just remember, you know, when you were there for me. When I was going through my shit. Before Jin died. And I want you to know that I'm here.

I don't look at TJ when he says this, so I can only imagine his face.

I start to open my mouth, but nothing comes out.

So I just stay silent.

And then the silence becomes its own physical thing.

Which is when TJ starts the car, again.

And we're pulling back onto the road, again.

A few months before he's dead, on a balmy November evening, Kai and I laze across his sofa. He's pretzeled himself around me while I tap at my phone, until his hands start traveling south, and I finally look up, and it isn't long before we're kissing, and then we're sucking each other off.

Kai finishes. I finish.

We lie next to one another, cradling each other's feet.

Then Kai burps.

Bitch, I say.

It's nature, says Kai.

It's foul.

Fouler than fellatio?

Pretty goddamn close, I say.

You know what's *really* gross, says Kai, and he shifts until his lips meet mine.

He tastes like me, and I taste like him.

I think, for a moment, that my life has been a too-long equation and this moment is the answer.

But then Kai burps again.

I laugh in this honking sort of way. Which hasn't really happened since I was a kid.

And Kai continues to burp, his own brass band, while I laugh along beside him, nearly falling off the sofa.

My last argument with Kai was a dumb one.

We'd just left some bar. I was walking way too fast. Pissed about something that I can't even recall. Kai told me to slow the fuck down, but I didn't, and I can't remember why, and I just sped on while he tried to catch up, and when he called my name I ignored him.

You're always fucking leaving, said Kai. That's your problem.

You're one to fucking talk, I said.

What I do is for *work*. It's to pay *bills*.

I don't even know what the fuck you do. Fucking translating? Fucking novels? Shouldn't you be in a fucking library?

Now you're being a head ass.

I'm saying that you're making a choice. It's a choice.

Fucking grow up, said Kai.

We went on like that, whisper-shouting from sidewalk to intersection to crosswalk. It couldn't have been longer than fifteen, twenty minutes. When I think of it now, it feels like days.

But when we made it back to our place, Kai asked me about the laundry. I popped into the kitchen to make him a sandwich. Everything was forgiven. Or even forgotten. Because that kind of shit just didn't last between the two of us.

Like we knew there was only so much time left.

Now we only ever argue in death.

Look, I say. You left first. You fucking won.

But Kai doesn't reply.

I try it again, and there's only silence.

So I say it again, louder. To myself.

The descent starts slowly, and then all at once.

An extra upper in the morning. A few pills at the bar before work. A fuck or four more over the course of an afternoon—I'm still functioning, mostly, but there's a haze.

I don't mind it.

One morning, Diego kicks his feet against the kitchen counter, jangling his keys.

We're late, he says.

We aren't, I say.

But the garbage guys already came by. And the dog walkers. And the recycling.

Sometimes they're a little early.

Jake says they're *never* early.

Absolutes aren't very reliable, Diego.

You just don't want to admit you're wrong, he says, rapping his knuckles on the marble while I pack his lunch.

When I finally look up at the kid, he freezes, folding his hands behind his head.

Also, says Diego, I never said thank you. For the other day.

That's okay.

Still, thank you. I was just having a shitty morning.

Don't say shitty.

Fine. Hard?

Hard, I say. And it's cool. That happens sometimes. You don't need to apologize because you didn't do anything wrong.

Okay, says Diego. Then you don't apologize either.

All I do is apologize, I start to say—and I don't.

One night at the bar, we're slower than usual when Fern stomps out of the office, steaming.

I have to go, he says. You two hold down the fort.

Is everything cool, asks Minh.

It's my son, says Fern.

Shit, I say.

No, says Fern. He's fine. Just acting out. He got in a fight. His mom's already at the school.

Minh and I glance at each other. Fern reaches over the counter, pouring himself some tequila. He downs it in a shot before he starts pouring another.

Is that a good idea, says Minh.

Fern seems to catch himself. And he drops his glass on the counter, stepping outside, just like that.

But the glass is still full.

I'm just starting to knock it back when Minh cradles my elbow.

You okay, fam, he asks.

Now I'm family, I ask. How'd I earn that?

I've always felt that way, says Minh, looking a little hurt. Whether you knew it or not.

Now I know for sure, I say.

I have a question though, says Minh, but he shuts up as two whiteboys in khakis hover by the register, chirping about vodka sodas and clapping their hands to the Selena video above us.

When one of the whiteboys meets my eyes, I hold contact until he blinks away. I can't remember if I've already fucked him or if I've only thought about fucking him or what.

Once they're gone, Minh asks, What are you gonna do when the bar closes?

That's not gonna happen, I say. Fern said we'll hold out.

I'm sure he meant it at the time, says Minh. And I'm not trying to be a dick. But two bars on the block have already folded this *month*, so—

Shitty, boring bars, I say.

Sure. But now they're gone.

That hasn't touched us, I say.

Yet, says Minh. I've heard it's only a matter of time.

For who, I say, and Minh purses his lips.

He sighs, shaking his head. Making this face like he's breaking bad news to somebody's kid.

So much for fam, I say.

I'm just saying, says Minh. I'd start making plans. I'm gonna start taking more classes. There's an apprenticeship gig for a disability services job that my cousin's helping me with. I can put a good word in for you, if you want.

He sets a hand on my shoulder, smiling.

I let it sit there, just for a second, before I push it away.

Convenient fucking time to jump ship, I say.

Minh's eyes widen. He mutters something in Vietnamese. And before I can apologize, he's already turning back to one of the whiteboys, who's bitching about how something's wrong with their drinks.

Later that night, back at Fern's place, I key in through the back gate. Fern's car is gone. I spy Jake on the patio with a cigarette. He's in basketball shorts and a sweater, and he flinches at the sight of me, but then his eyes settle. It's the first time I've really seen his body—it's average in a comforting way.

I ask if he's heard from Fern. Jake nods, ashing his cigarette.

That idiot kid, he says.

Kids fight, I say. That's nothing serious. And they fucking deserved it.

Sure. I heard about them being shitheads to him, but Diego's still being careless. The cops got involved.

What, I say, and for a second my stomach folds into itself.

Campus security, says Jake, looking up at me. Nothing wild.

You're sure?

I'm positive, Cam.

And Diego's okay? You've talked to him?

Yeah. Just fucking convinced he's in the right.

Oh, I say. Well. He is. And cops are garbage.

Jake gives me a look, then he smiles. I take one of his cigarettes, lighting up.

Diego's been going through something lately, says Jake. Probably puberty pains. But he won't talk about them with anyone, and the kid's mom says he barely even looks at her lately.

He's young. He'll come around.

Sure. Just like his dad.

I was the fucking worst growing up.

Is that right, says Jake, and he sizes me up, and I don't know why but there's a chill in my neck. All of a sudden, I feel the need to be in motion.

Anyway, I say, I thought nurses didn't smoke.

Then you haven't met very many nurses, says Jake.

I ask if he wants a cup of coffee, and Jake tells me he's fine. So I step inside, easing out of my sneakers, and then I'm back at the door, and I run into Jake as he's locking it behind him.

I really don't mean to kiss him.

It isn't something I've planned.

But it happens.

And we do.

Jake doesn't pull away, so we just stand there, kissing by the window, and I put my hand on Jake's belly and that's when he grabs my wrist.

Whoa, he says.

Shit, I say.

The two of us stand there. Frozen.

We still haven't really done anything.

A kiss can be explained away.

But then I feel for Jake's shorts, and he's hard. As I fold my palm over his dick, his shoulders jolt. So I close the distance between us, tugging at him, and Jake holds my other wrist steady, meeting my gaze when I try to move it, but then his eyes roll back, and the noise he makes when he comes is more like a sigh than a moan.

Which leaves us exactly as we are.

I don't know what to do with my hand.

But I don't give Jake time to say anything: I turn toward the kitchen, wash the mess off under the faucet, and then I'm out the door, before he's calling my name from the porch—and by the time I look up again, I'm already down the road, thumbing through my phone for a hookup, calling a Lyft to take me literally anywhere else.

A few nights later, Mae reaches toward me for a platter of fish, and she says, When was the last time you had a meal like this?

We're settled in the dining room tucked behind the bakery. It's the first time I've eaten in TJ's home since I was a kid. When I was younger, I'd walk over from my place, and Jin would've sat beside Mae, laughing with his arm around her shoulders. But now Mae ladles rice for me and her son, while TJ sits at the head of the table, hunched over his phone.

It's been a minute, I say. I usually do the cooking at Fern and Jake's place. Or we'll order takeout.

They're treating you all right, asks Mae.

Yeah, I say. They're a cute family.

They better be, says Mae, looking at me and then her son.

When TJ doesn't respond, Mae stares, smiling, until he finally looks up.

He winces at her, flipping his phone down.

A platter of smothered chicken sits between the three of us, beside a kimchi tomato salad and some pasta covered in rosemary. I'm regretting not popping a pill before dinner.

TJ sees me fidgeting. He stares at my hands until I kick him under the table.

He'll never tell me who he's texting, says Mae.

No one important, says TJ.

How would I know?

You wouldn't. That makes one less thing for you to worry about.

Mae doesn't look convinced, but she hands me another bowl, which I pass to TJ. He holds it in the space between us, locking eyes.

You didn't take any, he says.

I took plenty, I say. I'm stuffed.

No. I watched you.

You must've blinked.

Then try some more.

I just *told* you—

Don't be a dick, says TJ.

Boys, says Mae.

Her voice is terse enough to shut us up.

Mae holds our gaze until we've settled. Then she pours more wine into her coffee mug, twirling her food with a fork.

It's been too long since we've been together, says Mae. Let's make it a nice evening.

So TJ shoves the bowl of tomatoes my way. I scoop more onto my plate. Then I take bites from the spaghetti and the chicken, and it's all delicious, and the three of us eat silently, until there's something like a hum between us.

Is the bathroom still in the same place, I ask.

Mae points toward the hallway. I don't look at TJ when I stand. But once I've locked the door behind me, I turn on the faucet, and it's maybe another five seconds before all that food leaves me.

Afterward, I linger in the hallway while Mae and TJ whisper back and forth. They're clearly arguing about something. I drag my feet, clearing my throat to give them some notice.

And once I'm back at the table, TJ turns to his phone. When I reach for more tomatoes, Mae gives him this triumphant look.

He thought you didn't like it, says Mae.

That's not what I said *at all*, says TJ.

Right, I say. So who *are* you texting?

TJ gives me a flustered look.

I say, They must be important if they can't wait until after dinner.

I turn to Mae.

All she's done is purse her lips.

TJ just keeps eating, chewing in between us.

Maybe you should invite them over, I say. It's not like Mae would give them a hard time.

I'm happy to wait as long as it takes, says Mae, cheesing, and before I can say anything else, she asks if either of us would like dessert.

But TJ stands, knocking the table back a foot. I hear the patio door open and shut. He hasn't slammed it exactly, which only makes it that much louder.

Mae insists she can handle the dishes but I tell her it's fine. Once I'm done, I head toward the porch, and I start to check on TJ but I turn around at the last second.

Instead, I grab my shit and head for the driveway.

I'm slipping on my sneakers when Mae grabs my elbow. She's holding a piece of Tupperware wrapped in foil.

You didn't take any cake, she says.

And then: You really could've eaten a little more.

A beat passes between us. Some whitekids driving way too fast yell from their car window. I don't catch what they've said, but it makes me tense up. Mae doesn't even blink.

I'll save it for later, I say. Diego will love it.

Diego?

My boss's kid.

So you *do* like living there, says Mae.

It works for now, I say.

You still talk like Jin, says Mae, chuckling, and before I can do anything about that she rubs a hand on my back.

We really are here for you, she says. You know that, right?

I do, I say.

And *he* is, too, says Mae, nodding toward the house. You just have to let him go at his own pace. He took it hard when you left. It was a lot to take in at once, and I think he was lonely. Especially with everything going on. Jin passed, and right before that, you know, TJ got his diagnosis.

Mae turns to me, running a hand through her hair.

Sure, I say, but it's not like you've ever told him you know about him being poz, right?

No, says Mae.

Why?

I don't think it's my place. He's managing just fine. Taking his medication and everything else.

But I told *you*.

Mae pauses. She bites her bottom lip.

You did, she says. And I'm grateful, Cam. It gave me context. I could help a little bit, where I could, and I could hold space for him. And TJ will let me know when he's ready.

But maybe, I say, letting him know that you know would be another way of showing up for him?

Mae purses her lips at this, crossing her arms.

Would that be for his benefit, says Mae, or yours?

I already know how fucked up I sound. I know it's none of my business. And that some of that is my fault. And I know this wouldn't fix anything.

And, and, and.

Listen, says Mae. You don't need to stir the pot. He really missed you, Cam.

Never heard that from him.

Because you're too much alike, says Mae. You wouldn't even know what to listen for.

She gives me another look. One that's more forceful. But then it melts into something tender and Mae hugs me, pushing me toward my ride.

Kai and I rarely ever spoke about family. When we did, it only came up in passing: this thing reminded him of his mother, that one reminded him of his sister.

The last time was in bed. We'd just finished fucking, which had taken a little longer than usual, and I'd laid my head on his hip while Kai's fingers played with my earlobe. Usually, our block was all car honks and yelling. But it was silent for once.

What do you think they would've thought, said Kai.

Who?

You know who. Your parents.

About what, I ask. You?

No. Grown-ups love me.

Of course.

I mean about you being queer, said Kai. How would they have felt?

Kai's pressing turned firmer. I scratched the hair lining his ass.

That probably isn't what I'd start them off with, I said.

That's not an answer, said Kai, and he stuck a finger in my other ear, jiggling it.

Who knows, I said. I don't think they would've been into it.

But maybe they would've.

Doesn't really matter now, I said.

It'll always matter, said Kai.

Am I so bad at sex that you're bringing up my dead parents?

We just never talk about this stuff, said Kai, propping up on his shoulder.

The movement of his fingers turned gentle, almost cooing. They grazed my neck, and then my shoulders.

Let's talk about *your* family, I said.

You know how they are. How that went.

Then we can pretend, I said. If it makes you feel better, we can pretend that I met them, and they liked me. We can pretend that they accepted you.

This was enough for Kai to stop moving. I felt him catch his breath beside me.

Would that really be okay, he asked. To pretend?

It would. Even though you're a fucking pervert.

Can you be serious for six seconds?

With your hands on me like this?

Fine, said Kai.

He raised both palms, setting them by his hips. I peered up at him, reaching for his fingers, bending my neck.

Kai simply stared at the wall, and I started to ask what he was thinking, but then he looked me in my eyes, kissing my nose.

Then we'll pretend, he said. Let's make it a happily ever after.

Forever and ever, I said.

The moment comes and goes. But these aren't the memories of Kai that I dream about. Only his myriad deaths.

Kai falls down a mineshaft. He T-bones his car on a divider across I-59. He takes the wrong medication. He intervenes in a fight and he dies. He's caught in a movie theater shooting. He's caught in a grocery store shooting. He drowns. He dies every conceivable way that someone can depart from this life, and none of them have anything in common and none of it has anything to do with me.

One night I'm pouring drinks at the bar when a pint of beer topples across the counter. This whiteguy in plaid tells me to stop being so sloppy. I tell him to go fuck his father. I don't catch just how loud I am until Minh snatches my wrist, leading me into the office.

Once the door's closed, I kick a chair. Then I realize it's the only thing to sit on.

Minh watches me from the doorway, shaking his head.

Cam, he says. Are you good?

Very, I say.

You sure? Because you don't sound it.

Are you a doctor? You fucking finished school already?

I don't need a fucking degree to see you tweaking across the counter.

Minh leans against the door, taking me in. Actually looking concerned. That's enough to take me down a little bit.

Sorry, I say.

You're fine, says Minh. I'm just worried about you. We both are.

Who's *we*?

Fern too.

Yeah?

Yeah. For a while now.

I think about telling Minh what's been going on, with Kai and the dreams and the drugs and the fucking and how everything feels like it's smothering me at once, like I'm fucking suffocating from the weight of myself.

I think about what he'd say.

Nothing to worry about, I say. It's fine.

If you say so, says Minh, but he keeps looking at me.

Back at the house, Jake's waiting for me in his uniform. The second I'm inside, he takes my hand, folding me neatly across the sofa. We don't go out of our way to keep quiet, or to shut the blinds, and it's only a moment before Jake's on his knees, and when I ask where he wants me to finish he just smiles.

It's been this way for a week now. Fern's spent his evenings at the bar, reworking the numbers and pleading with Cecilia. He says they're on the verge of figuring things out. And Jake hasn't said a word about why he's fooling around with me, or where any of it's supposed to go, but the fucking's good, and it means I don't have to chase ass anywhere else, and that feels safer than being out in the world.

It's another thing to keep me from thinking about Kai.

Or TJ.

Or anything at all.

When we're done, Jake grabs paper towels for the two of us. Then he squeezes my balls, kissing my cheek before he takes off for work—and once he's gone, I sip from his coffee, slinking up to my bedroom.

Which is when, of course, there's a knock on my door.

Diego pokes his head in. The kid's still in pajamas. He doesn't say a word, but he sits on the floor with his back to the wall.

I don't know what to say.

So I start with the obvious.

I thought you were at your mom's today, I say.

Nah, says Diego. I came back last night. She had a date.

He runs a hand over his face, rubbing his eyes.

You don't have to say anything, he says.

What, I say.

I mean, we don't have to talk about it. But I know.

Diego folds his palms over his knees. I think about what I could even say. All of a sudden, the room feels impossibly cold.

That's not fair to you, I say.

I wasn't even supposed to be here, says Diego.

But here you are.

I don't think it's all bad, he says. And I don't think you're a bad person. Either of you.

That's mature of you.

I don't know. Someone in this house has to be the adult.

Right, I say.

What I don't add is that it shouldn't have to be him.

But the two of us stay that way. Shadows from the window revolve around us. Then Diego stands, stretching, before he steps out of the room, shutting the door behind him.

A few nights later, at the bar, Fern asks if Minh and I can stick around after our shift.

Just to talk, he says.

Sure thing, I say.

Nothing too wild.

I believe you.

And the rest of our night plays out. Business is slower than ever. Minh keeps eyeing me from the register, because we haven't really spoken since our chat in the back room. But he doesn't say shit about it, and I don't attempt to prompt him, and my phone starts vibrating so I scan it and there's a missed call from TJ.

I leave it alone though.

He knows where to find me.

The bar's been empty for hours before we finally close up shop. Fern pulls a trio of chairs by the stage, beside the speakers. I sit in one while Minh slumps across another.

Thanks for hanging back, says Fern. I apprec—

Hurry up and fuck us if that's what you're going to do, says Minh.

You know this was never gonna be an easy conversation, says Fern.

Just say what you need to say.

It's the most heated I've ever seen Minh get with anyone. But Fern doesn't match him at all. He just sits there.

Sorry, I say. I'm not following.

Minh and Fern both turn to me. They look at me like I'm nothing.

It's simple, says Fern. Cecilia's decided not to renew our lease.

Bullshit, I say.

I promise you it's true, says Fern.

You just *talked* to her, I say. She—

Informed me that she's loved working with all of us, but we'll be closing operations next month. She's leasing out the space to—

No one's re-leasing shit, says Minh. Don't fucking lie, or treat us like we're dumb enough to believe her. We're getting demolished for a fucking high-rise.

That's not set in stone, says Fern.

Doesn't need to be, says Minh. It might take a year or two, but it'll happen. And you agreed. All so your fucking kid can keep going to his fucking school.

Fern only narrows his eyes at this. He takes a deep breath, and then another one, before he speaks again.

This was inevitable, he says. You know that. And I know you know that. It's just numbers.

That's not what you were saying over the summer.

I was wrong.

That's *bullshit*. Plenty of bars in this area are hanging on.

They might last six months, says Fern. Maybe a year.

You don't know that, says Minh.

We both do, says Fern.

Then at least they'll have fucking fought for it, says Minh.

You'll be getting a severance cut, says Fern, turning toward me, and Minh swallows whatever he's about to say.

But I still don't know what to say about any of it, let alone this.

So I don't have anything for him.

When Minh asks how much money we're pulling, Fern tells him the number.

It isn't nothing.

How is that even possible, says Minh.

Cecilia's supplementing the total, says Fern. That's what I chose to fight for. Either I made a decision now, while we have a choice, or the call would've been made when we didn't.

The three of us sit in silence. Laughter filters into the building as folks amble back to their cars on Hopkins. Some cumbia wafts through our windows, and a cello sonata lingers by the intersection, and I recognize the passage—Jin used to play it in the bakery, humming along with the crescendos.

That's when Minh stands. His chair screeches across the tile.

Fuck this, he says.

And then he's headed for the door. When Fern calls after him, Minh only waves his hand.

Which leaves just the two of us.

Fern's breathing heavily.

I don't know why, but I try to make as little noise as possible.

As the sound of strings fade away, they're replaced by cop sirens. We listen to them drone.

Are you storming out too, asks Fern.

There's no point, I say. We're going back to the same place.

Then go home, says Fern. I'll lock up here.

But a funny thing happens when I make it back to Fern's house: TJ's standing by the curb. He's in front of his car, vaping.

And then TJ's walking up to me.

Quickly.

When he shoves me, I just manage to catch my balance, but not before he nearly pushes me off the sidewalk.

What the fuck, I say.

Did you tell her, says TJ.

Tell fucking who? What?

Did you fucking *tell* her, says TJ, pushing me, again, only this time I manage to grab his elbows, and the two of us land on the grass.

We push against each other like a couple of penguins. Kicking our feet and straining our backs. But we can only keep it up for a minute before we're huffing in the dark, staring up at the skies, and I realize it's the first time that I've seen Houston's stars in weeks.

TJ's wheezing beside me.

Did you eat a house on the way here, I say.

At least I'm not a fucking slut junkie starving myself, says TJ.

Fuck, he says. Fucking fuck.

TJ's in tears now. He's trembling. He folds his arms across his knees in the dirt.

I want to reach toward him. To hug him. But I'm not sure how he'd react.

What the fuck is *wrong* with you, I say instead.

It wasn't your place, says TJ. It wasn't your fucking place.

I didn't tell Mae shit, I say. If she found out you're a faggot, it's because you're fucking sloppy. It was a long time fucking coming.

But you told Jin I was poz, says TJ. You told him and Mae everything.

And that's enough to shut me the fuck up. For once, in this neighborhood, there are no cars on the road. It's late enough that even the street's smells have changed. They're grassier. Unclouded by smog or people or the city around us.

I didn't bring it up with them, I say. It wasn't my fault.

You had no fucking *right*, says TJ.

I told them because they asked me, I say. You were hurting after you found out. They didn't know what was wrong. I loved you, and I loved them, too, and I didn't do it to hurt you, but Jin was dying and he needed to know. We wanted to help you.

TJ doesn't say anything to that. We're both still sprawled on the grass. But then he starts to pick himself up, sniffling as he catches his balance.

You shouldn't have come back here, says TJ. You should've stayed in fucking California with your dead fucking boyfriend.

You don't mean that, I say.

I promise that I do, says TJ. I promise. Everywhere you go, someone fucking dies. That's all you're fucking good at. Your parents died. Jin died. And you got fucking Kai killed, too.

Stop it, I say.

You should walk around with a fucking disclaimer, TJ says. You should tattoo that shit on your fucking face. Let people know what they've signed themselves up for, fucking around with you.

Please. Please stop.

Fuck you.

TJ stares me directly in the eyes. His voice is steady. And then he picks himself up, hobbling down the driveway. When he pulls his car onto the road, he takes all of the block's light with him. But there are still the stars, just barely. Snarling down from above.

My final morning with Kai was entirely unremarkable—he was leaving that afternoon, for a trip out of town, and he wouldn't be back for a week. So we slept in. It was a Sunday. The two of us had planned on going out the night before—but we dozed off in front of *Mirai* instead, and when I woke up for coffee, the screen was still paused on a little boy reaching for his sister's arm in the sky.

Kai bumbled into the living room behind me. He rubbed at his face, searching the counter for toast, pushing away some stacks of pages he'd just finished translating. We took everything back to the bedroom, scrolling with the remote until we found *Pom Poko*, and then a documentary about jellyfish, watching the way they pulled and pulled and pulled and pulled and pulled without ever really leaving each other.

Our thighs glowed in the television's light. The fuzz of Kai's cheek scratched my neck. And we watched another pair of documentaries—about tuna shortages, about Tina Turner—before the two of us threw on some shorts for a walk to the corner market. The owner waved from the window. He rarely caught either of us solo. We grabbed a cucumber and also some parchment paper, but once we made it up to the register, Kai dipped back into an aisle for soy sauce and kombu and a bag of pecans. When he asked the owner if they'd gotten any shio koji, the man reached behind the counter for a bottle, swearing that he'd ordered some just for Kai, and a few weeks later I would stop by the same market and the man would frown when he saw me alone, and ask about Kai, and I said he was just away for a bit but the look on the man's face told me that he didn't believe it.

On our way back to the apartment, we passed a woman selling sunflowers. I asked Kai if he wanted any, and he said no. He figured they were probably old. And also we were shitty at taking care of plants: Kai never remembered to set them in water, and I took too long to throw them away when they died.

But still, I said. You love these.

True, said Kai.

So after I paid the lady for two bundles, I carried the groceries while Kai held both bouquets.

You wasted your money, said Kai, but he buried his nose in the flowers anyway.

I couldn't see his face for blocks. Just the petals bouncing over his gait.

TJ doesn't call.

Minh doesn't show up for work.

Fern acts like everything's business as usual and Jake brushes by my shoulder in the hallway in the morning, smiling.

I go to sleep and wake up and go to the bar and score T when I can, and sometimes I fuck whoever, whenever I can, and that's it.

Eventually, I cave and call TJ.

His phone rings and rings and rings.

We make Harry's closure public. First in the bar, and then on social.

Business picks up that night.

Two days later, we're packed from end to end. It's even enough to bring Minh back.

When I find a minute to ask how he's doing, Minh says, All good, like we've only just spoken that morning.

He goes out of his way to act like nothing's changed. But he isn't keyed in to how many sips I'm taking behind the register. And also how, every few hours, I find a new guy to fuck in the back of the bar for a few minutes, after a bump of coke on the sink and a tab in the back room, and then I'm back at the register before I'm back in the bathroom, and that's how the next few nights go until the lights finally pop on and I'm blinking myself awake for yet another fucking morning.

A few nights later, well past midnight, I've made it back to the house from the bar when Fern calls my name.

I'm already in bed, tucked away in boxers. The rest of the house is silent.

And I've just decided that the noise was a dream when Fern calls me down-stairs again.

So I find him standing in the living room. Still dressed from the bar. Jake's sitting beside him on the sofa, wiping sleep from the corners of his eyes.

I scan Jake's face, but I can't see anything crucial.

Or I don't know him well enough to know what to look for.

Sorry, says Jake.

It's fine, I say. Where's Diego?

At his mom's place, says Jake. But I told Fern this could've waited.

Look, says Fern. We're all adults here. I thought it was better to talk sooner than later. And there's no subtle way to ask this—

That seems to be a theme with you lately, I say.

We were just wondering what your next steps will look like, says Jake.

My next steps, I say.

Like your plans, says Jake. For the future.

Ah, I say. You're kicking me out.

That's not what this is, says Fern. We're asking because we care about you. We just want to see where your head's at.

Right, I say. So you're not putting me on the street because I fucked your husband.

Jake twists his hands. Fern gives me a look I've only seen from him at the bar.

Did Diego tell you, I ask.

What, says Jake.

Are you gonna blame the fucking kid for this, I ask.

I already knew, says Fern.

On the street beside us, or maybe the next one over, a cat starts whining. A woman tells it to shut the fuck up. Some other voices cheer it on, and when the cat finally stops, those voices all disappear at once.

Jake told me after the first time, says Fern. He asked me if it was okay. I told him it was fine. You're a pair of consenting adults, and you did it safely, and that's it.

That seems a little thin, I say.

I don't think so, says Fern. We've been open for a while now. You got off. Jake got off. No harm, no foul.

So you both fucking used me, I say.

No, says Jake, sitting up.

I'm not upset, says Fern. This isn't us punishing you. But it's been months, Cam.

Look, adds Jake. I'm sorry if I hurt you. I thought you knew this was all temporary.

We're not trying to sound like some unstable couple, says Fern, because that's not what this is. I really do think we're being reasonable. And you can tell us if we aren't. But we just think, you know, enough time has passed. Diego's getting older. The bar is closing. We should all start looking toward the future.

The two of them sit across from me, leaning on each other.

They really do look like a match.

Like something that'll last.

It's comforting. And horrifying.

All at once, I feel myself standing. I step toward them, setting one hand on Fern's shoulder and another on Jake's. They keep their eyes on me, and when I reach inside Fern's shirt, he gasps a little bit, and I feel Jake turn. Fern's still shaking while my fingers slide up his skin, rubbing his chest, and as I guide Jake's hands toward mine I feel something in the room shift. And then I'm on my knees, and Jake's kneeling beside me, guiding my head toward his husband's cock, until the three of us are moving in tandem with one another, pulling and sucking and tugging before we're all on the carpet, out of our clothes. Fern spreads his legs underneath us. Behind me, Jake pops in one finger, and then a second. Fern gasps when I enter him, and I jolt when Jake enters me, and I realize all at once that my time in their home has come to an end.

I'll start packing. I'll look for a new gig. I think about this as I listen for more sounds from the road, until the noises we're making and the words outside blend together, carried by the rhythm we've created, blending into each other and sinking under the drone of the city that towers above us.

And then and then and then and then and then and then and then the bar's closing party is the following evening.

It feels like the end of something.

I'm fucked up beyond recall.

Drunk and high as I've ever been. But it's also the most lucid I've felt in months.

When I turn the corner on the bar's block, slipping by arms and legs and between shoulders, the line seeps across the road and down the street next door.

When I make it inside, Minh's manning the bar by himself, with receipts stacked on receipts in his queue.

Where the fuck have you *been*, he says.

Everywhere, I say. And now I'm here.

I haven't spoken to Jake or Fern since I ditched their house in the early morning: I left after we came. I've simply stayed out, grabbing Lyfts. I found one hookup on Westheimer, and then another one on Taft. I ended up at the bathhouse on Emancipation. I saw the time and made my way to the bar but not before I found a house party fuckfest on the way by Hyde Park. It's raining outside, and the room is sopping, and the bar's the most crowded it's ever been, and I'm barely keeping up with tickets, so I hit the bathroom for another upper and I'm starting to feel my peak when I see Fern behind the bar, and there's nothing on his face that says he's booting me onto the streets or that I busted a load in his mouth last night.

He smiles and asks how we're doing.

I try to answer. I can taste the syllables in my mouth. But I can't get them out because I'm too busy trying to breathe.

Cam, says Minh.

Cam, says Fern.

But I can't and don't respond.

I can't really *hear* anything.

And then, out of nowhere, I hear everything all at once.

I don't know when the wheezing begins but once it takes hold it just fucking sits there, starting in my brain and sliding down into my throat, and then some fucking twink across the counter yells that I've given him the wrong drink so I ask him to wait a second, raising my hand, steadying myself on the railing, and then some other dude yells for me to close him out and another guy asks when I'm going to take his order and the twink calls me a bitch from his perch on the stool so I take the drink from his hand and I toss it in his face and it's enough for Minh to cup my elbow in his hands, asking if I'm okay, and I shove him even though I couldn't fucking tell you why, so Minh slips trying to balance himself and he falls on a group of customers just outside the bar and he hits his head, hard, and then a crowd forms around him, checking on him, and Minh waves his hand like, Yes, I'm fine, but he doesn't stand up, and a bunch of people have started taking out their cells and I hear Fern call my name so I swat one phone and then another and I walk through the crowd pushing pushing pushing until I'm out the door, back into the open air, and I walk through the blackness toward the road and then the lights, which actually belong to a pharmacy, and my breathing hasn't stopped and my head just keeps expanding, and I walk inside and to the back of the store by the cough medicine, where I can slump into the corner, and I can finally sit, and the one thing I can do is wrap my arms around my legs but I'm only there for like thirty seconds or just one minute or possibly an hour before this attendant approaches me, a Black woman, and she asks if I'm all right, and I tell her that I think I need help and she asks if I'm safe and I tell her I don't know and she exhales and slows her voice and asks if there's someone she can call and I tell her I don't fucking *know* so she asks me for my phone and I unlock it for her before I hand it over and another guy appears behind her, a whiteman with a name tag, and he tells me that he'll have to call the cops if I don't leave, and this woman tells him that he can't do that and he shouts that she isn't the fucking manager and then the two of them start arguing and I cover my ears because it's just too fucking *loud* and the only thing that makes it even a little quieter is more noise so I yell, too, until I see the manager finally dialing and the Black woman asking him to stop so I stand to leave and the manager tells me to sit but it doesn't matter because I've already shoved him and also the customers that have crowded around us, until I'm back on the road in the night and the dark again, headed toward more lights, walking toward traffic, and then alongside it, and then away from it, just walking until I'm somewhere along Washington, which is when I run into the first guy, and he yells at me but I'm not really paying attention so I keep walk-ing and this guy's people follow me, laughing, but they're getting closer and closer and then they're too close so I turn around and I shove one of them, once, and then once again, and I'm shoving them a third time and then a fourth time and after the fifth is when I hear the first *Faggot* and then I feel a fist on my face but honestly it feels so much like a kiss that I want to laugh, and the first kick is soft, and the ones that follow it feel even softer, so I take them for what could be fifty minutes or five hours or fifteen seconds and even when I know that they're gone I stay in a ball on the concrete just in case, until I feel the side of my face slick with itself, until I can't hear anything at all anymore, and by now it's dark enough that I can't see where I'm going, and I think that, eventu-ally, I'll step into absolutely nothing, which means I'll have to stop walking, and that would be it, but I don't know when that'll happen so I keep stepping and hitting solid ground and for a second it reminds me of how my parents would walk with me in the dark on the beach, just telling me to put one foot in front of the other, laughing along with the waves, but no one's laughing now and I don't know how far I'm walking but I keep going until the night swallows me whole because it's something to fucking do.

I'll only tell you once.

It was the weekend of Kai's second translation's publication. We hadn't gone out in ages. But I knew this was important for him, and that something had changed, so we made it a point to carve out time to celebrate. Kai had just made it back from a trip out of town, one he hadn't really told me much about, but when I picked him up from the airport he'd been glowing.

Clearly you won the lottery for us, I said.

Nah, said Kai. Even better.

He said he wanted to party. We planned to hit the clubs. This wasn't usually his thing, so I asked if he was serious but Kai waved me off.

Isn't that what people do when good things happen, said Kai.

There's no right way to celebrate, I said.

Maybe. But weren't you a party boy?

That's a past life.

Then let's live it up for a night. I want to feel how you felt.

That's dumb, I said.

Probably, said Kai.

We set tabs on each other's tongues. I made Kai pick a safeword. He scribbled it on his hand with a purple Sharpie and we drove to the bars, which were as packed as they usually were. We danced in the dark of the Abbey, and then the Eagle, before we huddled in the corner of Gaslamp, grabbing all over each other.

I was already flying high, but Kai told me he wasn't feeling it. It was late by then. Around two. Kai was giggly, wavering on his feet.

How are you feeling, I asked.

Lovely, lovely, said Kai. And also amazing.

Is that enough of a celebration for you?

That and then some, said Kai.

So I told him we'd call it quits while we were ahead. We walked back down Santa Monica to our car. The E fully hit Kai on the way back, enough to nearly knock him over, until all he could do was laugh, hugging me and kissing my cheeks, and I told him to keep that energy for when we made it back home. We'd taken his car, but I'd already planned on driving, and Kai asked if that was a good idea because we were only fifteen minutes from our place, and maybe it made more sense to call a Lyft, and I saw the cop car the moment we pulled out onto the road but my lights were on and I was below the limit and we were a few blocks away from the apartment when it finally pulled us over.

The cop had red hair. He asked where we were headed. Kai said, Home, but then the cop started talking to me. I asked if he hadn't heard Kai. The cop asked for my license and my insurance, except the car wasn't in my name and the cop asked why that was. Before I could answer, he asked me to step out of the car. Kai asked what we'd done wrong. The cop said it didn't matter. They were looking for some guys in the area and I fit the description. And I told Kai it was fine, and the cop asked me to step out again, and I told him to give me a second and Kai told the cop that this was fucked up and Kai reached toward the glove compartment, which is where he kept his registration, and I thought for a second about how I'd been meaning to add my name to the car, to the registration, but I'd just never had the time, so when I heard the first pop my brain didn't even register it. I thought a tire had gone out. Then there was the second crack. And a third. I knew what had happened before I *knew* what had happened. And Kai made a wheezing noise like he'd sucked up all the air in the world, and I started to unbuckle my belt when the cop told me to put my hands on the wheel. I didn't want to, but my body made me, while Kai wheezed beside me, and then he started crying, wheezing, and I started crying, wheezing, and Kai started laughing just a little bit, giggling his safeword, a sound like a child or a very old man, like he'd finally discovered the secret of the world and it wasn't all that impressive after all, but then he stopped.

It's hard enough living in the world, says Kai, let alone being honest about it.

He sighs, folding his arms behind his head. He's in a Gudetama T-shirt and boy shorts. I've never seen him more comfortable.

But I like that you're trying, he says. That's good. It's a start.

Then he smirks, snorting.

I don't know what time it is or where or what I am when I feel the nudge on my shoulder.

All I know is that the rain's finally lulled. And I can't see shit in front of me, but some guy in running shorts and a windbreaker hands me an umbrella. He shivers while I stare at his legs, and then his torso.

I think he's sort of cute.

Then I recognize this man in the dark of the night and it's TJ.

Nice calves, I say.

Thanks, says TJ. I've been working on them.

Standing above me, he looks taller than I know he is. But then TJ settles beside me, and I make a little room for him. We sit while water pools around us, funneling into the bayou.

How'd you find me, I say.

Some lady called from your phone, says TJ. And then I pinged your watch.

Bullshit.

Not at all.

You've known where I was.

I've always known where you were, says TJ.

So when I ran into you at the bar, I say. The very first time.

Yeah, says TJ.

Okay, I say, and then the two of us sit in the silence with the rain.

I realize that, somehow, I've made it all the way down Shepherd. I shift from the pain.

TJ says, Fuck, Cam. You're bleeding.

It isn't bad, I say.

It's a lot worse than not bleeding.

I'm not dead, I say, and TJ opens his mouth to say something else but then he doesn't

When he touches my arm, I scream. And I mean it. And I laugh to drown it out. So TJ drops his fingers, but he tries lifting me again, easing his shoulder through the crook of my elbow.

I think we should leave now, he says.

I don't have anywhere to fucking go, I say.

I'm laughing. I can't help it.

TJ doesn't say anything to that.

Instead, he stretches, showing a bit of his belly. Then he uses the wall as leverage to lift the two of us up.

It hurts. But we manage.

TJ slips his jacket over my shoulders.

We start our walk from under the bridge.

The sirens behind us don't sound any closer, but they don't disappear either. It could just be the backdrop of the city. Houston's natural state.

Aren't you still pissed at me, I say.

I'm fucking livid, says TJ. But let's just worry about getting you into some socks.

I watch the bottles and the cans and the bags sifting through the water. It all goes somewhere, even the shit that gets caught in the tide. But TJ leads us out of the bayou, and we walk until we've made it to his car, parked by the Kroger down the block.

You don't have to do this alone, says TJ.

Okay, I say.

I can be there, too.

Okay.

That's when TJ opens the door for me. He slips into the driver's seat himself. It's still pitch-dark as he flicks on the ignition, turning onto the feeder road, but the only thing I can hear is the sound of my crying, for the first time since Kai died, fucking gasping on TJ's chest, but he wraps an arm around my shoulders and we're the only light on the road as TJ brings the two of us home.

Kai

Glass reflects less than 5 percent of the light that strikes it. Hana told me that in a bar beside her apartment in Shimokitazawa. I'd just finished translating her second novel: the first one hardly sold in Japan, but it was a bestseller in the States. And this thing she told me drunk struck me harder than anything of hers I'd worked on.

When I asked where she'd heard that, Hana laughed, flicking her cigarette. Her mother had told her. The woman had been a ceramicist. She'd died by her own hand a few years prior. Hana had dedicated the first book to her.

Hana told me that she'd hated her mother, but she still kept all of the woman's pottery in her apartment. When I asked why, Hana said, *Because it's beautiful.*

The publisher flew me to Tokyo to work with Hana on her edits. We'd been given a three-month deadline. But she and I spent most of our days in tiny dives around her neighborhood instead. We rode bikes past the financial district. We ate dinner with her ex-boyfriend, a stocky guy with dyed hair who blushed at the sight of me. The rest of the time, I slumped in the sento beside my rental in Setagaya, wading in the bathwater beside salarymen and shop owners and bankers. Sometimes I worried about what I'd have to show for my time, but Hana waved me off if I brought that up. She said this was why she liked me.

For the next year, whenever I entered a bathroom or a bedroom or somebody's living room or whatever, I'd find the mirror on the dresser or the closet door and wonder what it was hiding. And what I wasn't seeing. I stared at the glass until it showed me something new.

But I only saw what I could see. Didn't know what I was missing.

●

If you're Black and you're a translator then people look at you funny. They get this fold right over their nose. You can't see it unless you're looking for it. But if you're looking for it, you can't unsee it.

If you tell these people that you translate Japanese, their folds intensify, crinkling like aluminum.

After Hana's first book was published in America, I attended the requisite book parties. I told the other attendees I was an actor. Or an adjunct. Or a DJ. These responses got me handshakes and hugs. No one knew any better.

Sometimes these same people mistook me for the venue's staff. Sometimes the venue's staff mistook me for the staff. If I corrected any one of them, they'd look at me like, Okay? And?

This kind of made sense to me. I grew up in Louisiana. Just like my mother, and my mother's mother, and her mother, too. My grandmother cooked for the family that owned her mother. My mother worked in a restaurant four miles from the house they'd lived in. It was owned by that same family. This wasn't something we spoke about.

. . .

On our second date, Cam asked me to cook for him. He called it an act of love, and I yelled at him, No no no no no no no no no no no no no.

We walked along the sidewalks in Echo Park, and sometimes we held hands but mostly we didn't. From time to time, Cam's hands would graze a flower in the fences beside us, starting to pull by the stem, but I always stopped him. He never asked me why I did it. But he stopped.

Eventually Cam started cooking for me. He called me the first boyfriend he'd done this for. A lie I didn't feel compelled to challenge. But Cam spent Sunday mornings hunched over a cutting board, layering dough flap over dough flap, slicing meat, folding it all into each other.

This shocked me. He looked like some guy off the street, and then there's this fucking Michelin spread.

The smell of chicken turnovers woke me up in the morning. Cam leaned across the counter, crimping more pastry folds with his fingertips. I thought about how, when I was a kid, the smell of grits and eggs on the stove stirred the same electricity in my head.

When I asked where all of this knowledge came from, Cam shook his head and said, *A past life*. Maybe that should've annoyed me, but it didn't. Because I got it. Everyone comes from somewhere.

Still—it made me laugh. Cam would ask why I was chuckling. And I couldn't really explain it, but that's how our relationship worked: one of us was always laughing, and the other never really knew why. Which wasn't a bad thing.

. . .

We kept laughing. That's my point.

Maybe time was more of a mirror than a circle. Revealing 5 percent or less.

•

In Baton Rouge, the land between my childhood home and the airport was all barren grass and browning concrete. There weren't many houses on our block. The ones that still stood were all sunken in.

The only green in the area came from my mother's garden. She had a plot for her eggplants and her peppers and her squash and her okra. Some sunflowers stood by the window, peeking out over the sill. Her other flowers sat in another patch, sequestered to grow on their own.

Our neighborhood was mostly one-story shacks. They were abandoned after the last hurricane. The only other buildings were the sugar plants and the liquor stores, and there was a bus route that would bring you to New Orleans twice a week.

My sister Bree called this the vortex. Even with maximum escape velocity, you got pulled back in. Didn't matter how far away you made it. Or how far away you *thought* you'd made it. Gravity was the law and that law was universal.

Eventually Bree made it to Dallas for her nursing degree. She disrupted her theory for a while.

Growing up, I had a friend named Olly and he believed in the vortex, too. His dad had gotten caught in it. And also his brother. They worked at the sugar plant but Olly swore he was getting out. He wanted to be a sports agent, and he had a plan to make it happen. We lost touch after high school so Olly still existed inside that dream to me. Another disruption to gravity.

The lies I told growing up in Louisiana were my first acts of translation: Yes, I'll stay. No, Officer, nothing's wrong. Yes, I'll bring home a girlfriend soon.

State offered me a scholarship to study sociology. A counselor at the high school sent my application. I couldn't tell you what *the study of the development of human society* meant, but I accepted.

It was the closest thing the entire university had to Japanese. I'd always wanted to learn the language. Its rhythms fascinated me. There weren't many things that did. But when I told my mother what I wanted to do with my life, she blinked and asked if I could even find Tokyo on a map.

And what about my grandchildren, she asked. Then it was my turn to blink back at her.

My family taught me the difference between acceptance, allowance, and understanding. Also: just being. Sometimes they overlap. Usually, they don't.

On the rare weeks I came home from college to visit my family, we cooked. Bree washed the collard greens. I skinned the potatoes. Our mother washed the chitlins in a tub on the front porch. We cooked enough food for twenty people.

When I asked why we'd prepared so much, Bree told me to shut the fuck up. It was one thing for me to never come home, and another for me to critique when I did. I said that if I couldn't ask questions, then I simply wouldn't come back, and Bree said, So fucking *don't*, and that's when my mother shushed us both.

My mother would say, *Cooking is care. The act is the care.*

In this way, she was a translator, too. We misread each other.

Yes, I'm going to commute from home. No, the university says I can't leave campus or I'll lose my funding. Yes, I'm coming home for the holidays. No, I'm only staying a few more weeks. No, I'm not sure when I'll be back.

. . .

Years later, when the publisher matched me with Hana, she emailed me a photo of the town where she'd grown up. It was just outside of Fukushima. Nothing but empty buildings, still barren from the disaster. I magnified her photo on my screen, splicing one of my mother's house beside it.

It was hard to tell where one photo ended and the other one began.

I sent that back to her.

When I woke up the next morning, Hana had emailed our editor. She'd approved me for the job.

•

The first guys I fucked were at State. They had absolutely nothing in common and no plans to come out. You would think this might make finding dick difficult but it did not.

One whiteguy I fucked wanted to be a doctor. Another one worked with numbers. One Honduran guy worked at a grocery store, and a Canadian guy worked in communications. Then there was a Cambodian man who wanted to be a masseur, like his father. He touched parts of my body that I hadn't known existed, activating creases that I hadn't known were there.

Another whiteguy I fucked was a father of two. He told me we could meet at his place, but then I got there and we stood in the garage. His kids were eating dinner with his wife in the backyard. I thought about leaving right then, simply disappearing, but I didn't.

The best one lived in Lafayette. He was an Indian guy about my age. He said he'd go half on a hotel, and it was an hour before he showed up to the Hilton, but I waited, and he fucked me until minutes before we had to check out.

Around that time, I was working on a transfer to UCLA. They had a modern languages program. It was fully funded. A Black woman I studied under at State helped me with the application. The acceptance rate was less than 10 percent, but she told me that didn't matter.

That summer, I was back home from college. I'd stopped cooking with my mother. She didn't fight me on this, but Bree called me a punk and a motherfucker.

My sister was working on her nursing degree in Texas. She still made time for the twelve-hour round-trip drive to Louisiana every weekend. She asked when I was going to start doing my part, and I told her I was trying and Bree called me a fucking liar.

A few days later, I heard from Olly. Texted entirely out of the blue. I drove my mother's car to his place across Baton Rouge. He lived near a row of nail salons and strip clubs beside the highway.

Olly's apartment was mostly just a laptop and a dinner table and some speakers. His mattress sat on a carpeted floor. Each room smelled like incense and roach deterrent. The sofa was torn from end to end. When I asked Olly who he'd gotten it from, he cocked his head and cracked his knuckles. That sofa is what he fucked me on.

Afterward, we smoked Olly's shitty weed on the same sofa. He told me he'd made it to school in Alabama. That hadn't worked out. Tuition was too expensive. He'd enrolled in BRCC once he made it back home, but one day he got stopped for a broken taillight and then he forgot to pay the ticket. The next time he got picked up, he was arrested. And now he couldn't land a job. But the sugar plant was hiring, because the plant was always hiring, and Olly could either do that like his father and his brother or work on an oil rig like his cousins or he could sell blow.

He lay with his head on my belly. I drew circles around his ear. Olly said, Must be nice to come and go, and then he blew a smoke ring in my nose.

When I made it back to my mother's place, I helped her with dinner. I washed the greens. I massaged the meat. I cooked the rice and deveined the shrimp. Bree was suspicious but we ate without incident.

While we washed dishes afterward, Bree asked what my deal was. I told her it was nothing.

Then I told my sister that I couldn't stay.

I just can't, I said. I'm sorry. But I can't.

Bree kept scrubbing at a dish. It was already clean.

Then she said, You're just like him. I always wondered which one of us would turn out that way.

Do you think you're better than us, said Bree. Do you think you're better than any of this? Did you think, for even a second, that they'd look at you any differently?

And then Bree said, Don't you fucking tell her.

I heard back from UCLA that evening. The light was dim on my phone's screen. I read the email's subject and I set my phone facedown, and I walked outside, and I sat on the dirt, spread out across the land.

. . .

Years later, I found a similar scene in Hana's book: her protagonist splays face-down in front of her childhood home. She makes snow angels in the grass, covered in soot. But still—the woman turns around and stares up at the sky, wondering after the stars.

At first, that sounded too sentimental to my ears. Then I thought about Bree. And also my mother.

When I asked Hana if a memory had prompted the scene, she told me that wasn't important. She called it a description. It was only fiction.

•

I met Cam at a bar in Silver Lake. I'd gone with Shun, my roommate in LA. Shun and I had met at UCLA, and he'd landed me my first paying translation work, flipping instruction manuals from Japanese into English: pamphlets packed with toasters, car engines, coffee machines, anyone who'd have me.

I didn't have a car in California yet but sometimes I walked as far as my legs could take me. I wandered under awnings. Through parks. Along-side neighborhoods covered in fronds. Our neighbors were Korean and Mexican and Black, and regardless of the time of day they always waved back.

If I thought about the distance between Los Angeles and Baton Rouge, my ears popped. So I tried not to.

Shun spent half of his time in Japan, translating pamphlets for Honda. He pressed me to move abroad with him. Swore that we'd find more work. And also, Shun had a boyfriend in Osaka.

. . .

I told him I wasn't looking for a man. I just wanted to work. And Shun rolled his eyes every time, knocking on wood.

One night Shun and I passed through a house party in Atwater. After that, we caught a ride to Akbar, before we made our way to the Eagle, and Shun stepped away to buy drinks, but once he stood up Cam took the empty stool beside me. I don't even think he meant to.

The truth is that Cam glanced at me like I was nothing. But his elbow brushed against mine. So I asked who he was, and where he was from, and Cam blinked under the lights before he told me he worked for a bank. When I asked why, Cam said that's where they kept the money.

His bluntness felt like oxygen. When Cam asked what I did for work, I told him about translation, about Hana.

You're the first translator I've ever met, he said, yelling into my ear. *Everyone in this city's a translator*, I said. *Okay*, said Cam, *then you're the first one I've met who's managed to do it for money*.

He gave me his number and said to call him for lunch. I told him it might be a minute, and Cam asked if I had a boyfriend. *I'm not a whore,* he said. *We'll eat lunch, not dick.*

The next morning, Shun and I flew to Itami International. On the plane, a beautiful flight attendant asked if he was my tour guide.

•

I slept in the spare room of Shun's boyfriend's apartment. He lived on the seventh floor of an Osaka walk-up, tucked away in Tsutenkaku. Sunlight filtered through the windows every morning. I smoked cigarettes on the patio, watching seniors stretch in the park.

. . .

One day an old man saw me staring from above. He waved.

Shun's boyfriend's name was Oda. He was nearly six feet tall. Sitting at the coffee table beside him, Shun and I looked like children. But Oda laughed easily and often. He worked in an office, and the three of us took our dinners together around the city. Sometimes we visited shrines and went for long walks. Bumping shoulders on drunken walks home, we laughed at the sight of us.

Hana's next book held an astounding amount of cooking. Characters cooked to center themselves. They cooked to show their love. They cooked when they were wasted and when they were horny and when they were sunken into themselves. When I asked Hana what prompted the emphasis, she told me it was a different way of seeing.

We never cooked in the apartment—Shun and Oda couldn't, I simply wouldn't—so in the interest of accuracy I bought pots and pans and utensils of my own. It'd been such a long time since I'd touched these tools that they felt raw in my hands. At one shop, I brought six different versions of the same knife to the register. A woman behind the counter smiled, replacing everything I'd picked up with something better.

I spent hours at the stove translating recipes, attempting to re-explain them for someone like me. I bought so many Band-Aids from our neighborhood's conbini that the Korean-kid salesclerk reached for them whenever I walked by.

Shun and his boyfriend took bites from the dishes I made. Sometimes, it was just that: one bite. Eventually, they started lingering, waiting for leftovers.

. . .

I thought of my mother, who simply stood up from the kitchen table in the afternoons, only to sit down having made eight dishes with twenty-four flavors and varying textures.

We weren't really anything yet but sometimes Cam texted me. Little things, like: How are you doing? What's the the weather like? How's work? But also: What was your favorite color as a child? What's your favorite sound in LA? What's your favorite time of day to look at the city's skyline?

I read these messages during the daytime. Which was well past midnight for Cam. This was thoughtfulness or chaos, but I didn't care to ask which.

That isn't to say I was chaste: the local guys I fucked were usually one-night stands. We'd meet at love motels in Doyama. More than a few had girlfriends. One or two were married. But we'd lie next to each other after we'd finished, snaking our limbs together before we finally separated.

One time I hooked up with a guy a few years younger. He asked if we could cuddle afterward, just for a minute. A few hours later, I woke up with my arms wrapped around myself.

On my way out of the love motel, the cashier only raised an eyebrow. It was too late for the trains to run. I walked an hour back to Oda's place. I found him and Shun asleep in front of the television, and I wedged myself beside them, and Shun threw a hand over my shoulder before I fell asleep again.

When I told Cam about Hana's book, he told me to send him my progress. That afternoon, I passed through the conbini, and the Korean clerk informed me that he was clocking out forever. When I asked where, he said Seoul. He'd made up with his girlfriend. I shook his hand as he handed me an egg salad sandwich.

. . .

I told Shun that I'd sent Cam my manuscript. He sat in the bath washing his hair. I spread out beside him next to the tub, passing him more conditioner, and when Shun laughed, I asked why. He said, *You've never asked me for relationship advice before.*

A few nights later, Cam sent me a sound file. I could hear him tapping his screen, adjusting his desk as he spoke into the phone—then he read the manuscript I'd sent him aloud.

His reading voice held an easy cadence. He hardly tumbled from page to page, only stumbling over the Japanese phrases. Every once in a while he'd clear his throat, pausing for water.

Halfway through the recording, I slipped on my clothes and walked to a bar. It was owned by this couple, and the husband's English was better than mine, and they always waved through the window when I passed them on the street. After I ordered a beer, I pressed play again.

I see what you mean, said Cam.

This part's a little confusing, said Cam.

But here's the fun part, said Cam. And then he laughed.

•

The first time Cam and I slept together back in LA, we both came twice. The second time I finished, Cam spread the mess between his fingers. He drew a circle around his lips, laughing.

I didn't ask if he was fucking anyone else because I already knew. Sometimes, I'd blink at him, wondering if he was sober. But then we'd go for a walk, and Cam would point out a star, or a sign, or a weed in the concrete. I figured this was just how he was.

. . .

When Cam told me about his parents, and how they'd died, his delivery made me wonder if he'd been asked many times or if he'd never been asked.

It's a thing that happens, he said, slicing a loaf of bread. He made a splat sound with his tongue.

I'd spend two months in Osaka and the next two in LA. Shun and Oda decorated my days in Japan. Then I had Cam in California. Sometimes I wanted to step back and look at my life, but I thought if I did that it would all just disappear.

One day while I was in Osaka my editor asked if I was open to a promotion. Before I could answer, she added that it would include a longer stint in the Kansai regional office. I'd be on-site all year, working with other authors, too. She told me to think about it.

A few days later, Bree texted me. I was on the train platform beside Oda's apartment. Some kids blew bubbles beside me, and their mother kept shooing them to stop. When our train arrived, the family stepped inside, but some bubbles still lingered as they sped down the track.

My mother had fallen down the stairs. In her first message, Bree told me what happened. In her next one, she told me where the hospital was.

In the last she wrote, If you can find it in your schedule.

One thing I'll never forget is how Oda left paper cranes around his apartment. Years ago, he started having panic attacks. They came without much warning—on the train, in the office, at home after midnight. A friend recommended that he find something to ground himself, and that's what got Oda started. His windowsill was lined with birds. Before he and Shun left me at the train station, he'd slipped one in my bag for the flight.

So much work to make them stay in one place, he'd said.

•

My flight from Osaka to Tokyo to Toronto to Houston to Baton Rouge took forty-nine hours. When I stepped outside the airport, the air was so thick that I gagged. A bald security guard flirted with a woman behind me, fiddling with a packet of gum.

Bree picked me up from Arrivals. From the way she spoke, you'd think we were the type of siblings who talked every day. She told me about being a nurse practitioner in Dallas. She told me about her boyfriend. She described her white patients' faces when she gave them their prognoses.

Maybe that's how you feel with your books, she said.

My mother waved from her hospital bed. She asked why I'd come all the way from god knows where for a fall. Bree told our mother that this wasn't her decision to make, and the doctor, a Chinese guy with warm cheeks, followed our words like a tennis match.

In the hallway, a Cuban nurse took Bree and me aside. Her voice was low and calm as she said that our mother would never walk without assistance again. And also, a year of therapy. Then she added, It's good that you're local. Most people don't have that.

We took our mother home the next morning. The neighborhood had changed since I'd been away. But the closer we drove to the house, the buildings began to dwindle, and the concrete grew patchier, and dirt gave way to grassless fields.

Men lingered under the lone stoplight. When my mother nodded from the passenger seat of Bree's car, they nodded back.

My editor told me to take as much time as I needed. Shun told me to take care of myself. I started to call Cam, but I left a voice message instead.

He responded immediately. Asked how I was doing. But his message was the only one I didn't reply to.

•

For the next week, Bree and I fried toast and bacon for breakfast. At noon, we sliced oranges and pan-fried tomatoes. When evening fell, I'd step outside with a bin to wash the collards, dragging another washtub across the concrete to dry the greens.

The houses in front of ours still sat empty. When I was younger, I'd squint to see if anything was inside. Maybe a bat. Or a gang of wolves. Or a witch that'd hid for decades.

Whatever I'd built in the world felt like it was starting to disintegrate.

My mother said, If this is what it took to bring you home, I'd have thrown myself off the roof sooner.

One night, Bree watched me sauté onions with chopsticks when she said, What exactly do you do for work again?

I told Hana that there'd be a delay in my translation. A few hours later, she sent me another photo of Fukushima. It was her family's porch, stuffed with potted plants. She'd taken it during her last trip home. I held it up to the window by my bedroom, to see where her porch stopped and my mother's began.

. . .

The clothes in my closet were all too-short shorts and oversize sweaters, but I needed a cigarette and I'd left my vape carts in Japan. So I walked to the corner store. It stood about a half mile away. An old man at the register stared at my thighs as he rang me up. In the parking lot, another guy told me to turn around, but I kept walking, and he called me a faggot, and I kept my eyes on the moon, and I didn't look down until I saw the porch light where Bree and my mother sat outside.

No no no no no no no no no no no no no.

My mother was in bed when I stepped in the yard for a smoke. It wasn't long before Bree joined me. She asked for one, too.

A few minutes later, I told her I couldn't do it, I couldn't stay the year.

Bree stood as silent as the evening around us. Then my sister said, Fine. A few months will work. You'll stay until I can take the time off. We can split the burden.

I told Bree I was leaving the next morning.

I can't, I said. I just can't.

We stood smoking. The sky turned a shade of dark blue I've only ever seen in Louisiana.

Bree said, You really are your father's son.

When I told my mother I was leaving, she hugged me. She was still mostly asleep. A little woozy from the painkillers. She whispered something in my ear, but I didn't catch what it was.

•

An old Mexican man nudged my shoulder on the plane to Los Angeles. A cup of hot tea sat on the tray between us. I thanked him, and then I asked why he thought I drank tea. But he only shrugged in return. He'd been watching *Spider-Man* on his phone.

Shun sent me photos of the trees by Oda's apartment. The leaves were changing, growing from a muddy nothing into a vibrant pink. Winter had been colder than usual, and most of the foliage had died, but some tiny flowers had bloomed into themselves, frail to the touch. He picked some of them, setting them in jars along the counter.

Cam met me at LAX. He started speaking when I grabbed my luggage from baggage claim, and I could hear him, but I chose not to listen.

Even still, Cam chatted as we sped from I-105 to I-101 toward the apartment. He talked and talked as I lugged my bags up the stairs, until I told him I needed a moment in the shower, locking the door behind me. I heard him exhale from the other side. He sounded relieved.

When I stepped out of the shower, I found Cam in the kitchen. He wore the face you make when you aren't sure what happens next.

I passed him in my boxers, ducking into the refrigerator. I pulled out cabbage and eggs and scallions. I stood over the cutting board, and then the stove, and when I'd finished, I sat across from him. We both picked at the pancake with our hands, until it warmed our faces, too.

TJ

2.

After Cam checked out of rehab, I invited him to help with the bakery. This was a while back. Just before the pandemic shut shit down in Houston. Probably wasn't the smartest fucking thing I've ever done and I've done a lot of dumb shit.

3.

Lately we open at seven. The bakery closes shop around three. Stays busy six days a week but we'll take Sundays off unless there's some rich-bitch private event. Jin used to keep the place open on weekends, sliding aprons over our necks and whisking egg wash over our heads. But he's dead now so we changed the schedule.

4.

Our menu's seasonal on paper but we sell just about everything: tarts and breads and cookies and croissants and cakes and pies and puddings. Sometimes we've got hotteok. Songpyeon and mooncakes, too. But kolaches are where we make real money: these were Jin's delicacies. It's how he learned to break even with a Korean bakery in fucking Texas.

And kolaches reminded Jin of summers he'd spent growing up in Busan. Every afternoon, back when he was a teen, some half-Polish baker saved him sausage pastries on his walk home. But a few decades later, after a bunch of other shit happened, Jin met Mae at a protest in downtown Houston. He literally collided into her friends. So when Jin found those kolaches again, in the neighborhood of the woman he loved, on the morning after their first date, he called it fate.

5.

If it sounds like bullshit, that's because it is.

Probably.

Either way, it's what Jin told reporters, and of course they smoked that Light-Skinned Immigrant Had A Dream And Found His Way shit up.

When Jin died, everyone told this same fucking fable at his funeral. They cried about it. Laughed at all the right parts. Chewed on the kolaches I'd baked for the evening with their dumb fucking faces.

Then they drove home with their mouths full and I never saw most of them again.

6.

The pandemic fucked us like everyone else but we've managed better than most. We ended up in the fabric of a lot of people's day. Despite everything, pastries were a treat you could give yourself. They had an immediate payoff. Some sweetness alongside the bullshit. And they were cheap.

Now we get white people from all over Texas. Mae's been talking about hiring more people to help but we've been too fucking busy.

7.

At first I could manage the load. Ivan's our shipping guy, but he did whatever we asked him to do. Fati handled the register. Mae was—and is—adamant about masks and distancing, so we never had too many people standing around, and we could sell our shit through the window when things got really bad. We did a decent job of getting people through the door.

And then there was Cam.

Those first few months he was useless. Paralyzingly slow. Constantly trashing his workspace. Cam added too much flour to the kouign-amann. He over-mixed the muffins. He burned the fucking butter. One morning when I handed him the recipe for Danish dough he looked up at me and cocked his head and said, This isn't how Jin did it.

Are you out of your mind, I said.

I know it's your show now, said Cam, but—

Exactly, I said. You are a guest. Please do what the fuck I'm asking you to do.

That was enough to leave Cam standing in place, holding the recipe, blinking.

Ivan whistled beside us, laughing through his mask.

You're like my nephews in Chivas, he said. Always roughhousing.

That isn't helpful, I said.

8.

Also: Cam's different now. Some of it must have been rehab. And some of it was probably Kai. But I think the shift must've already been inside of him: a weed in the concrete that finally found wiggle room.

He sticks to a routine though: Cam's up when I am. He works during the day. He closes out and he cleans and he spends the rest of his week napping with Mochi or pretending to read or hanging out with Mae. He's got a therapist he sees weekly that's been helping with his eating. And Cam journals in the evening, even though he swears that he hates it. Keeps the same dumb smile on his face at all hours.

I don't really get it.

It's a complete one-eighty from the guy I knew.

One time I asked Mae what the hell they even talked about. She gave me this weird fucking smile before she pulled up some photos on her phone, asking which ones looked best for the bakery's IG.

9.

A few weeks after Cam moves in, Fati corners me by the register.

Tell me the deal, she says. But don't lie.

He's a family friend, I say.

I *said* not to lie.

Here we go.

So you aren't fucking him?

Do you fuck your family friends?

I fucked a friend and now he's my husband, says Fati.

But Usman's great, I say. The last good straight man.

He's fine, says Fati. Don't change the subject. Cam seems fuckable enough though.

Everyone is if you squint, I say.

And he *lives* here, says Fati.

For now.

That wasn't the question. I have eyes. So where does he sleep?

On the game room sofa, I say. Did HPD put you up to this? Are you a CI now?

I'm just trying to decide how sorry I should feel for you, says Fati, running a hand through her hair, a curly brown mixed with strands of blond.

She started working for us a few years back. Over the course of one month, Fati quit her father's Sugar Land dentistry, married her live-in boyfriend, and immediately declared that she was only interested in polyamory. She showed up at our place a week later. Fati celebrated all of this by dyeing her hair. She's maybe the most astounding person I know.

But now she smirks at me under her mask. I don't need to see her entire face to know what it's doing.

Save your sympathy, I say. Cam just can't live on his own right now. So we're helping him.

That I get, says Fati. You're doing a good thing.

Goodness has nothing to do with it, I say. We're short-staffed. Direly.

And yet you still fight Mae on hiring.

You've been spying on us?

I have ears, yes.

We can handle it.

You *think* you can handle it, says Fati. That's one of your problems.

I ask if she's been making a list of them. Fati's face lights up.

Fetch me the notebook with enough pages, she says.

10.

After Jin's funeral we arranged his altar in the living room. The next thing Mae did was strip his name from the sign on our roof.

Mae smoked beside me as we watched a contractor pry each letter off. I thought she might cry or sigh or throw herself into the dirt but she just stood on the lawn directing everyone toward the compost bins.

That night, Mae sat on the floor outside my bedroom. I hadn't spoken to her all day. Hadn't known what to say. And it fucking confused me that she looked more at peace than I'd ever seen her. It was a subtle thing, a loosening in her shoulders.

You're sad, said Mae.

You're projecting, I said.

But you're still sad. It's not like we're changing the name. We just don't need it hanging over us.

It's fine.

You're very convincing, TJ.

Whatever.

Have you eaten?

That wouldn't fix a goddamn thing.

Language, said Mae.

Sorry, I said. Fuck.

Then Mae said: I miss him, too.

Doesn't seem like it, I said.

What you can't see with your eyes might surprise you. But we'll take this place and make it our own.

It's already different. It can't be the same.

That's what I'm betting on, said Mae. If you'll help me make it better, then it will be.

11.

That shut me up.

I hadn't planned on staying or leaving.

Hadn't planned at all.

When I was a kid, I thought I'd take over the bakery from Jin and Mae.

Cam would help me.

We'd live together and make it work.

Which sounds like a fucking fairy tale now.

But those stories are what they are because of idiots like me who believe them.

12.

So I stayed in the Heights.

I worked at the bakery.

Mae and I managed to hold on to our regulars. Jin's absence made them wary, but they knew us. Or they knew Mae. I'd started taking classes at HCC—for programming—which should've taken me out of the rotation, but I worked my ass off and did both.

We revamped the house's storefront. I spent my mornings baking. I failed one class. And then a second. One of my whitelady professors asked why I was burning cash just to sleep in her course. I folded croissant layer after croissant layer after croissant layer until they came out right, and Mae said my food tasted like Jin's, which made her happy, so I threw that shit out and I started all over again.

Eventually, we were bringing in as much cash as when Jin was alive.

Then we started clearing even more.

13.

A year passed.

And then another three or four.

We saved enough money to flip the whole bakery and Mae gave everyone raises and one day I dropped out of HCC.

My world was fucking small but it was mine.

14.

Cam called this the weak way out. Staying. Maybe it is. But if Cam isn't weak— if whatever the fuck he's going through is strength—then all I can say is that it's not what I'm looking for.

15.

A little after midnight, I'm leaving my room half-naked for a shower when I find Cam lounging on the game room sofa.

That's where he's been crashing. Tucked under a weighted blanket with the cat. And he looks up from his phone, lingering on my ankles, and then my knees, before I watch as his eyes travel.

But then Cam sighs.

He turns back to his cell.

What the hell, I say.

Just haven't seen your body in a while, says Cam. It's sturdy. Thick.

Fuck you.

Clearly not.

This is something Cam does: he suplexes you with indifference.

When we were kids, he'd grind whatever you cared about into indiscernibility. He'd shake his head. Wave his hand. Sigh. Groan.

I admired the hell out of him. He was thrilling to watch. Because I hadn't known people could do that. But it's completely different seeing it used against me.

What are you even still doing up, I say.

Candy Crush, says Cam.

I'm serious.

Of course you are. That's sweet.

Cam flips his screen to me then. I see bodies lined up across the app's grid. They're smiling and half smiling. Eating dinner and throwing peace signs. Forming fuck-me frowns and lazing in hot tubs and handstanding on beaches and glowering in work photos and hugging their friends in graduation gowns and bending themselves over bedposts.

Cam scrolls through them all. Entirely aimlessly.

I'm only window-shopping, says Cam.

Is that safe, I say.

They're filtered by vaccination status.

That's not what I mean. Should you be doing that?

Doing what?

You know what I'm saying.

I want you to use your words, says Cam.

The two of us stare at each other. Out of nowhere, a shadow passes over Cam's face.

And then he smiles.

Dick genuinely bores me at the moment, says Cam. But I appreciate your concern.

Okay, I say. As long as you're good.

A better question is how are *you*, says Cam. We never really talked about that.

The bakery's fine. You're here every day just like me.

We're talking about you, says Cam.

I'm gucci, I say.

Right, says Cam. That's the problem.

He clicks his tongue, turning back to his phone.

Are you still seeing Ian, he says, not looking at me.

No, I say. Not really.

But that's who you're flushing yourself out for, says Cam.

If you're Ronan fucking Farrow then why the fuck did you ask?

To see what you'd say.

I'm still trying to figure out what this has to do with you.

I just want you to be careful, says Cam.

I *am* fucking careful, I say. Obviously I'm undetectable. I get tested for STIs twice a month. You literally can't get more careful than me. I'm *literally* the safest person you could have sex with.

Your body isn't the only thing that can be hurt, says Cam.

Six months in rehab and you're the poster boy for emotional safety, I say.

The words pop out before I can stuff them back in my mouth.

I expect Cam to look hurt.

Or vengeful.

Or for his eyes to expand until they explode, roasting me in the process.

But none of that happens.

Cam sneezes instead. Mochi snuggles farther into his armpit.

Work, he says, tapping at his cell.

And then, turning his screen my way, Cam says, Are you on here?

Do you want to die, I ask.

Is this you? This black square? BreedMyHole42?

Just fucking go to sleep, I say, nearly tripping down the hallway, just barely catching my balance.

16.

A few hours later, I'm stoned on Ian's sofa while he fishes two beers from the fridge.

His place is a Sixth Ward walk-up. It's a short leap from the bars downtown. And we're watching *Parasite*, for the fifth time, when Ian reaches for my thigh, initiating the short dance of his ending up inside me. Which he nearly is, with his hands on my stomach and my fingers on his back—until I grab his dick and he gasps, exhaling, and says, Sam.

What, I say.

Shit, says Ian. Sorry.

No, I say. It's fine.

That wasn't cool. I—

You're fine, I say. It just caught me off guard.

We try restarting our momentum.

Ian tongues my thighs.

I can't get hard again.

It's *fine*, I say. We're fine. Maybe I need a break.

We've only just started, says Ian.

Just give me a minute, I say, and Ian pulls a fugly face.

But he slips himself back inside his boxers. And I adjust myself, too.

I promise I'm not a fool. I've always known I'm expendable to him. And it's not like I've ever wanted a monogamous situation anyway—I already know that isn't for me. But, sometimes, it felt nice to pretend that he was somebody who was *mine*. And that I was *his*. It felt a little less ridiculous than it sounds.

For a few months, it was Adrianna and Kiera. Then there was Terry and Jen. For like a year and a half, Ian dated Isabella, but he called her Izzy as a pet name.

And then there was his ex-fiancée, Samantha. She's an accountant in Montrose. They were just about to fly off into the Acapulco sunset, for a happily ever after, and I was prepared to give up on our situation entirely—until one day, out of nowhere, Ian told me that she'd broken it off.

He hadn't seen it coming. Neither had I. When I asked Ian what happened, he didn't answer the question. But the night that he told me she'd left, he fucked me for something like eight hours, until his sheets were a puddle of sweat and cum and my back was sore for a week.

When Ian makes it back with more beer, he sets mine on the coffee table.

We watch a storm onscreen force tenants from underground apartments, flooding the road with their belongings.

Without looking at me, Ian says, I've been seeing Sam again. It's been happening for a while now.

What's a while, I say.

Since the pandemic kicked off.

That *is* a while.

Yeah, says Ian. Well. I couldn't just leave her alone. One thing led to another.

We sip our beers in silence.

I know I've got a handful of options.

I could stand and grab my gym bag and leave Ian to himself.

I could call him a bitch and a motherfucker and a punk.

I could block his number and delete him right the fuck out of my life.

It would take less than three clicks. We have no friends in common. No overlapping routines. He practically wouldn't exist anymore.

But Ian sets his hand on my chest, rubbing.

You know what, he says. We should go somewhere.

In the light of day, I ask.

That's enough to bruise him. But I can't help it.

Just for a weekend, says Ian. Maybe Galveston?

I hate beaches.

Then Austin. It could be fun.

Galveston would be better. I haven't been in years.

My parents have a condo out there, says Ian, sipping his beer.

I start to ask if he isn't worried that we'd run into them.

But then I use my brain for a second.

It'd just be nice, he says. To be out in the world with you.

And this is how it always happens: he says the exact thing that settles me, brings me back in.

He doesn't even mean to do it.

I don't know how to respond.

So what I do is set my beer on the wood floor, getting down on my knees. I'm wearing this red jockstrap Ian likes—once he spots it peeking from my hip, he reaches through my sweats, squeezing my ass.

Austin sounds great, I say, and the sound Ian makes when I take his dick into my throat is a single vowel. The most common sound in the English language. But it's one that I've never gotten tired of hearing.

17.

I met Ian at a bathhouse. This was a few years back. I'd pass through on weekday afternoons, when the halls weren't filled with circuit gays and muscle queens, and it was always the same faces except for when it wasn't—old guys and young guys and twinky guys and bigger guys and furry guys and waxed guys. I met a few football players. Some actors. Occasionally I saw porn stars, and one of them looked at me like I was a receipt. Another one fucked me delirious.

But for every new face, there were nine that I'd seen before. These guys looked the most comfortable. They drank Fanta in the hallways. Watched women's soccer by the lounge. Cracked jokes with the staff, slapping each other's backs and squeezing each other's elbows.

They always said hello to me. We'd chat about nothing for hours. I was already poz by then and, sometimes, when the club was mostly empty, I'd sit naked in the patio's heated jacuzzi wondering if these would be the best nights of my life. That didn't seem too bad at all.

One afternoon, this tattooed Black dude trailed me around the maze of rooms for an hour. He was taller than me. Thinner, too. Eventually he split off, and I ran into a different guy who insisted on rimming me, and after that I passed by the vending machine for a Coke, but I didn't have enough quarters and the tattooed guy clinked some coins against the wall behind me.

Just take mine, said Ian.

That was his opener.

I turned to him, squinting.

He looked different in the light.

No thanks, I said. That's a little familiar.

More familiar than getting eaten out by some stranger?

I leaned on the machine, adjusting my towel. Ian laughed, slapping the quarters into my palm, folding my fingers over them.

I only need one, I said.

Then you score yourself another Fanta when we're finished, he said.

Who says we're doing anything, I said, but Ian's fingers grazed my waist, and despite myself I was hard and we stumbled back to his room.

After he fucked me, we sipped Cokes on the mattress. The bathhouse's crowd had thinned out. Shit was silent except for the occasional stray moan.

Ian told me that he taught. When I asked where, he smiled.

I asked if he was married.

Not yet, he said. But someday. Soon.

One of those answers must be true, I said.

There are many possibilities in this life, said Ian.

Who's the lucky guy, I asked.

She's a woman, said Ian.

Oh.

And I'm the lucky one.

Clearly.

I'd finished my Coke, but I kept sipping from the can. That gave my hands something to do.

Are you open, I asked.

Meh, said Ian.

Is the marriage arranged?

No.

So it's a god thing?

Shit no.

Does she know you're bi?

We make each other happy. That's it.

Then what brings you here, I said.

Guys like you, said Ian, squeezing my nipple.

My stomach started to turn. I wasn't sure why.

Guys like me.

So I reached for my towel, standing to leave.

Wait, said Ian. You were great. What if we met again? Like, somewhere else? Would you be into that?

Is this how you do it, I asked.

I'm only asking a question, said Ian.

And why the fuck would I go anywhere with you, I said.

Because I like you, said Ian. You're adorable.

Mm, I said.

Can I at least have your name, he asked.

I smiled, but I didn't slam the door behind me.

I got dressed and drove to Taco Cabana and sat in my car. The meat didn't help my stomach. It just kept rumbling. And I couldn't figure out why, but then I felt my leg again, and Ian's imprint was still there, and that's when I realized that I never actually came, so I beat one off in the driver's seat, used the wrapper to clean it all up.

18.

A few days later, classes restarted at HCC. This was before I'd given up. I was slumped in the back of the room. I'd seen an email about a change of instructors, but I hadn't read the entire thing and of course that's when Ian walked in.

I wanted to melt.

I wanted to combust.

He stepped behind the podium, setting up his desk. Ian called roll and when he reached my name I told him that I went by TJ.

He looked up, blinking.

And then he smiled.

TJ, he said.

I crossed my legs under the desk. His voice made me harder than I'd been in weeks.

Some people set the key of their lives inside you and simply turn.

Stupid, stupid, stupid.

19.

I told Cam about Ian a few months later. We'd made a habit of texting every couple of days.

The first thing he said was: Fucking finally.

you don't think it's weird, I asked.

It's not like yr getting married, said Cam. He's engaged?

correct.

To a man?

nah

Ofc. & they're open?

idk if she knows

Exactly. So fuck it. Go wild. This guy's not serious about you, you're not serious about him.

i'm actually taking him kind of seriously.

yeah, said Cam.

But, he added, you know. It'll end. Right? He's trade. You'll have your fun and you'll find someone else.

Then he sent eight eggplant emojis.

I didn't know much about his life in California—after his graduation in New York, with the fancy finance degree and the bank job he finagled afterward, sometimes it felt like we had less to pull from. Sometimes he'd talk about his clients, or a shitty boss, but he mostly kept quiet. And whenever he asked about my situation in Houston, I didn't know what to tell him: it was the same as he'd left it. Nothing had changed.

But I knew Cam had a boyfriend. I knew his name was Kai. Cam told me he was a translator, and when I asked what that meant, Cam started talking about some other shit, and how I needed to start seeing other guys that actually wanted to see *me*, and I kept fucking around with my usuals and my one-offs, but I didn't find anyone else long-term, seriously, and eventually Ian's name stopped coming up between us.

20.

Back then, I still called Cam every few weeks.

I was the only one who ever reached out.

And then, months later, one of the only times he picked up the phone, Cam called me an idiot for sticking around with Ian.

You're in a fucking hole with that guy, he said.

That's not what you were saying before, I said.

Because I didn't think you'd still be fucking him, said Cam.

You thought he'd get bored with me? Like you did?

Fuuuuck. Really? That's what you're thinking about?

You said it.

And you're being a child. I thought you were smarter than this.

Why do you even fucking care? You're not even fucking *here*.

We were both yelling by then. My palms were sweaty behind the phone.

Clearly you're the fucking genius between us, I said.

At least I'm smart enough to keep my shit wrapped up, said Cam.

21.

After that, it felt easier to just stop talking altogether. He'd already stopped visiting.

22.

Then Jin died.

23.

Mae insisted that Cam hear about it from me. And I told her I couldn't do that, because he didn't fucking deserve it, which made her livid.

But Mae only asked once. And she didn't bring it up again.

The next time I reached out to Cam was after Kai was killed.

24.

At the last minute, I thought about hanging up. But it didn't matter. The phone just fucking rang and rang. When Cam's voice mail clicked on, he sounded exactly the same, as if nothing had changed—giggling like he was in on the joke, telling whoever was calling to try writing him a letter instead.

25.

Lately, the three of us eat dinner together. Mae sits at the head of the table. Cam and I fill out the rest of it. Which isn't too different from when we were kids, except that Mae hardly cooks anymore, and none of us really knows what the fuck to say without Jin filling in the silence.

He'd handled most of the cooking. Mostly Korean dishes. Or whatever Mae was feeling for that evening. But when Jin died, we didn't have a home-cooked meal for weeks—on the rare nights Mae managed something, it was dishes that reminded her of her husband: kimchi jjigae and juk and tteokbokki and butter rice with grilled mackerel.

Then I started cooking, too. I knew I'd never replicate Jin's. But I wanted to get as close as I could. Still don't know why. And that's when Mae ascended from the kitchen altogether, convinced that she had no business doing it with a man in the house.

And also she could tell that I liked it.

Which confused the fuck out of me at the time.

But it doesn't change the fact that we don't have shit to talk about at the dinner table.

Mae makes the face she always makes.

Cam taps at his phone, squinting.

I figure there'll never be a good time to tell them.

I say, So I think I might be gone this weekend.

Mae stops chewing. My stomach bubbles.

Is that right, says Mae.

Just for a few days, I say. To Austin.

What's in Austin, says Cam.

I just haven't been in a minute, I say. It'll be nice to get out of the city.

That's when I turn to him.

He doesn't even blink.

It *is* pretty nice this time of year, says Cam. Not too hot. Hardly humid.

That's what I'm banking on, I say.

We've got those interviews this weekend, says Mae. You'd be missing out on that.

Then I don't have to go, I say. It was just a—

Slow down, says Mae. I was just letting you know. You *should* take a break. Be scarce for a while.

Vitamin D is good for you, says Cam.

Exactly, says Mae. We'll hold down the fort.

I look between the two of them. They're both working hard not to grin my way.

Thanks for your approval, I say, standing with my bowl, making a beeline toward the sink.

26.

Three memories of Jin stand out for me and the rest have faded to bullshit.

They're all just blended colors.

Or shades of things that probably happened.

I recognize the outlines, but I can't call them by name.

27.

The first one's a little hazy: We're entertaining neighbors over dinner. Something we always used to do. This is before Mae and Jin opened the bakery, before money found the Heights and turned every other block pale.

Jin still sold cars. Mae worked at the real estate office. With Jin's fam in Korea, and Mae's in Atlanta, neither of them had roots nearby. So without any relatives around, they'd cook for the block most weekends, inviting whoever needed a meal to join us and hella people did: Cam's parents, Cristina Rodriguez's parents, the Ayutthaya fam, and LaTrice with her kids, and Adriana Ochoa and all the Argentinian folks living in the house on the curb.

Sometimes they brought their own dishes. Someone always brought music. Kenny Macias gigged with a mariachi band, and he'd bring his guitar and his buddies and they'd sing in the evenings. Jin grilled beef, steaming pot after pot of rice, and then there was the summer that he discovered crawfish, when every other weekend became some sort of boil.

Our place stayed packed until midnight. Mae never turned anyone away. And I was in the center of that, sitting in whoever's lap or dancing on the patio or standing beside Jin, holding his hand, while he told some joke or guffawed in his booming way.

Jin wasn't a large man but he expanded when he laughed. Made each room a little wider. Everything became warmer. Once he finished giving his attention to whoever was looking for it, his eyes always looked for mine, and when he met them he'd smile.

28.

I tell Fati about Austin before I take off. We're on break, smoking at the park, where the bayou and the public track meet I-45's edge. Ivan's holding down the register. Cam's fucking around in the kitchen. A few benches away from us, in a spotty patch of grass, a Black dude pumps his arms toward the sky while three exhausted white women do their best to mimic him.

With his torso facing the women, the man gives me a look. And then he does it again. His muscles are so clearly defined that it gives me a headache.

So your boy toy's taking you out of the cellar, says Fati.

You're less cute when you're rude, I say.

Then please tell me how to describe your relationship that isn't a relationship.

How's it any different from your situation with Usman? Don't y'all have your own things going?

Sure. Deliciously. But we do our laundry and sit down for dinner afterward. We babysit for our fuck buddies. Everyone's in the know. Neither of us hides each other under the bed.

That's very hetero of you.

Bullshit. I'm saying that we don't take each other for granted.

We're only going out of town for the weekend, I say. That's all.

No, says Fati. This is a significant thing, TJ. I just don't know if it means the same thing for both of you.

Our trainer has the white women doing planks now. Each of them looks like they've just discovered oxygen. Behind us, some Latinx kids skateboard past, yelling about pinche something, and the women look concerned but none of them allows their knees to fall.

When I offer Fati some of my pot, she shakes her head.

Promised Usman I'd chill on that, she says.

The good wife, I say.

Fuck you. It's the least I can do.

I dangle the vape pen in front of her. Fati bats it away.

You're not listening to me, she says.

I heard you.

And what do you think? Are you okay with Ian parading you around whenever he feels like it?

It's just a trip! There's nothing to *think*.

His girlfriend might say otherwise, says Fati.

Fiancée.

That definitely makes what you're doing more honorable.

The trainer beside us is drenched in sweat, but he doesn't drop his smile. Hasn't even grimaced. One of the white women wobbles her knees, groaning, and her partners attempt to hang on.

You need to be careful, says Fati.

I am fucking careful. We're safe.

You're so smart about everything else, says Fati. But—

Please, I say. Just let me have this.

It's not a lot, I say. And I know that. I'm not an idiot and I don't need you pitying me. But he matters to me.

I see Fati start to say something, but she stops herself.

Then she grins, reaching for my pot.

Everyone is something to someone, she says.

A second white woman drops to her knees. The third one is red-faced, fuming from her nose, before her legs hit the grass with a thud. And their trainer holds his pose for another thirty seconds, just because he can, before he gently lowers himself, too.

Then he turns to us. Again.

He nods at Fati, winking at me.

What the fuck, says Fati.

Ignore him, I say.

Do you want me to introduce you?

No.

Think about it. That's who you could be fucking. I've heard trainer dick is phenomenal.

No.

You could be just like those women, says Fati, blowing smoke in the air. At least you'd have a better shot.

29.

It's nearly midnight when our flight lands in Austin. A brown dude waits for us by baggage claim. He's holding a whiteboard scribbled with Ian's name, beside mine, smiling at us like we're newlyweds.

Which is when Ian makes an expression I can't read.

What, I say.

Nothing, he says. You're just my favorite.

So I'm one of the fucking gang?

It's a club of one.

Stop bullshitting, I say.

But Ian holds this face while we speed across Austin's express lanes. He wears it as we weave through traffic downtown. And it's there as we give the concierge our names, and a whitelady behind the counter warily asks if we need an extra key.

Our room's on the top floor. It's larger than the entire bakery. We set our luggage down, and Ian puts his hands on my shoulders. He's a few inches taller, but I make a point not to look up at him.

I won't suck your dick until you tell me what's wrong, I say.

Jesus, says Ian. Nothing's *wrong*. It's just that we're here. Together. You know?

It really shocks you that I came, I ask.

Everything about the world surprises me, says Ian, and his hands drop to my elbows, before they graze my waist—and then Ian's kneeling on the carpet, running his hand up my shirt.

We don't have to do this right now, I say.

I know, says Ian, continuing. But it's a thank-you.

For what, I manage.

You already know, says Ian.

Our luggage sits by the door. We're both still in our sneakers. Ian sucks me off, fingering me with one hand and squeezing my thighs with the other, and I brace myself with the counter but my knees can't help but buckle.

I can see the city's skyline through the windows behind him. It's mostly all black but a murky red creeps through.

30.

The next memory of Jin is clearer: One day, Cam and I were smoking by the cul-de-sac. He'd found someone willing to sell us some weed, in the way that Cam always seemed to find the things he wanted. These were the first afternoons I ever spent stoned, flat on my back in the grass, bumbling from end to end of the Heights.

This was after the accident with Cam's parents. Mae and Jin sat me down before he moved in, asking if I objected, and of course I didn't have a problem with it. Cam was my best friend. And my only friend. And he'd spent enough time at our place already. After our first few nights together, it felt like he'd always been there. We could finish each other's sentences. Or we didn't have to talk at all.

You could hardly separate us. We were in our own universe.

So we missed the men until they stood directly behind us: a pair of white-guys stuffed in suits. Snorting and crossing their arms.

One of them asked where we lived.

Before I could answer, Cam said, Around.

And do you think you should be here, the other guy asked.

This is our neighborhood, said Cam.

Never seen you before, said the first guy.

You know this is *my* fucking house, said the other guy. You know you're on *my* fucking property?

The man reached for my shoulder. Cam swatted him away. And before they could do whatever they'd intended to do, I felt palms on my neck and a shadow behind me, and the shadow belonged to Jin.

He told the men that we were kids.

We were *his* kids.

And the men turned to each other.

They looked at Cam.

Neither of them looked at me.

Then the first one shook his head, nodding the other one to his truck. Before they drove away, he rolled down his window, and as they yelled after us Jin took off his shoe and threw it.

Afterward, Jin drove us back to the bakery. Sat us down on a pair of stools. I thought he'd lecture us, or tell us off, or at least ask what the fuck we were thinking. We smelled fucking dank.

But he bent toward the two of us with a pair of chocolate-chip cookies. Set them in our palms. Jin watched our faces until we both took a bite, laughing when we said, Whoa, delicious.

31.

Our first day in Austin starts without a fucking hitch: We nap by Barton Springs. Walk down East Seventh in search of tacos. Ride scooters up Sixth Street until we're sticky with sweat. Back at the hotel, we haven't even locked the door before we're on top of each other, with Ian's hands in my shirt and my fingers in his pants, and he fucks me in front of the window, and for the next hour I don't care how I look or about the faces I'm making or the noises coming out of my mouth.

It's hours later when we're back outside and calling a cab. We walk on cracked concrete, bumping ankles and shoulders. It's the closest I've ever been to Ian out in the world, but when I ask if we can pass through a gay bar Ian snorts under his breath.

Fuck, I say. Never mind.

That's not it, says Ian.

And then he says, Why not?

That's a yes?

Call a Lyft before I change my mind.

So we make our way to Fourth Street. The line for one bar loops around the block. We opt for a smaller, smokier one instead, and Ian orders drinks for the two of us.

But Ian flirts with the bartender. He drags us toward the patio for the music. When another guy brushes his shoulder, Ian looks up and laughs, looking entirely comfortable, and it feels like I've been cheated out of something, like there's this formula I've been working with but it's been fucked this whole time.

When the track above us flips to Fleetwood Mac, Ian smiles with his whole face.

You doing okay, he asks.

Just magical, I say.

I'm lucky.

Yeah?

Yeah, says Ian. To be here with you. It means a lot that you came.

Don't be dumb, I say, blushing.

32.

The third memory of Jin that sticks with me is the clearest: It's late afternoon. He's already at work. It's also summer, and I can't drive yet, which means Cam and I are stuck in the bakery all day—and I'm sick of the kitchen, but it makes me sicker that Cam enjoys the labor.

Before moving in with us, he'd only hung around the kitchen. Within a few weeks, Cam was waking up early to prep. Then Jin started showing him the ropes. Cam picked up everything instantly. It wasn't long before he became a reliable baker, and Jin never put me down or compared us, but sometimes I'd glance at his face and I knew.

It's the sort of thing Jin values. And Cam doesn't fucking care. When I ask why he bothers, Cam doesn't even look at me, batting a kolache between both palms.

He says, You'd be stuck doing this shit by yourself otherwise.

So the two of us spend those weeks stuffed in flour and dough.

But it's also the summer that Cam and I start touching.

It starts slow at first. And I'd hardly call it fucking. One night, Cam simply crawls into my bed from the living room sofa, huddling next to me, and I let him. His fingers are always cold. It isn't long before they cradle my torso. I don't turn around to face him, but I let Cam jerk me off, and just before I come I muffle myself against a pillow.

We don't talk about it during the day. But not out of shame, or anything like that. Even if I don't have the language for it, I've known I was queer for years. And I know Cam's different, too. But also that he's more experienced than me. I'm just not exactly sure how that happened.

The next evening, Cam returns to my bed. He reaches for me but this time I actually grab his wrist. And he looks a little shocked, but I pull at his shorts when he starts to leave, and the sound he makes when I stroke him that first time is one I haven't heard since.

We start touching every evening.

We work in the bakery during the day.

Between the summer's humidity and the newness and the repetition, every moment rolls into itself.

And then, a few weeks later, we're sucking each other off when my bedroom door slams itself open.

When I finally look up, Jin's standing in the doorway.

His expression isn't malicious. But Jin isn't a malicious man.

What stays with me is the resignation behind his eyes: what I now know is confirmation of a thing he knew to be true, and hoped wasn't.

33.

On our last night upstate, I ask Ian if I can fuck him. This was his big taboo. He'd only ever topped me. And it wasn't something we'd ever talked about— since the first time we had sex, he just assumed that I would bottom.

We've changed into hotel robes, lounging on the mattress. I've cracked open a window. An orchestra of frat kids filters upward from below.

Ian just blinks at me.

Oh, he says. You're serious.

Affirmative.

We haven't done that before.

Double affirmative.

I stand in front of Ian, nudging open his legs. The robe creeps up his skin, separating at his groin. And I push his knees farther, and then farther, until I'm looming over him and his gown falls all the way open.

We're bumping up the marriage, says Ian.

Wait, I say. What.

Sam and I, says Ian, staring me right in the eyes.

He says it like he's asking what we should order for room service.

I plop onto the mattress beside him.

When, I ask.

Soon, says Ian. The end of the year.

You didn't need to tell me this today.

I'm sorry, says Ian.

You could've kept this shit to yourself, I say. You couldn't have fucking waited one more fucking day?

I just thought—

You had to fucking ruin this one fucking thing! Like I'm just this piece of fucking meat—

I wouldn't be here if I thought that, says Ian.

He's loud enough to shut me up. It's the most exasperated I've ever seen him.

I'm here right now because I want to be, he says. You're a part of my life.

And yet it's still happening, I say.

I didn't say I was fucking happy about any of this!

But why, I say.

Because you deserve to know, says Ian.

I fucking hate that word, I say. No one fucking *deserves* anything.

Neither of us is touching now. Some man shouts drunkenly in Mandarin down the hallway. Then another guy's voice softly croons just beside him, and you don't have to see them to know that they're holding each other.

I've always been honest with you, says Ian. This whole time. You if no one else.

That's not what this is about, I say.

That's *all* this is about.

You're a fucking coward.

And here you are, says Ian, in love with a fucking coward.

I open my mouth.

Then I close it.

Ian looks pitiful. I wonder if this is a side of him that his fiancée sees, too.

And I know, definitively, that I'll never see him again.

So I wipe my face, close my robe.

I duck into the bathroom.

I run the water, and I sit on the floor, and it could be thirteen minutes or three hours later but eventually the door opens and Ian sits beside me.

He doesn't say anything. But he hugs his arms around his knees.

His pinky inches toward mine.

When he grazes me, I let him tug at my hand.

And then I make a decision.

He's tight when my fingers enter him. The look on his face is so surprised that I almost laugh. And Ian doesn't loosen up quickly, but eventually he does, moaning beneath me, until we fuck with his back propped against the tub, and before I can finish, Ian says my full name.

It's only the second time he's ever done that.

And I fight the urge to say his, too.

But I can't even fucking stop myself from doing this either, and eventually it comes out.

34.

Cam didn't call me the week of Jin's funeral.

It'd be bullshit to say I expected that. Despite whatever the fuck was going on between us.

I'd managed to numb myself from everyone else's words—Jin's friends, and his siblings that came to the funeral from Busan, and his siblings that didn't, and Mae's parents, and Mae's brothers, and our neighbors, and everyfucking-body else.

I wondered what Cam would think of them. I knew he'd probably call bullshit. And I wondered if he'd call me and my silence bullshit, too.

Sometimes, it felt like I was waiting on him to let anything out.

But he didn't call the first week.

And I didn't hear from him the week afterward.

The rest of the month passed and we still hadn't spoken and Jin was still dead in the ground.

Then one day, walking out of the kitchen, I heard Mae on the phone.

I watched her from the hallway.

And then I heard Cam's voice, too.

And I felt warm.

And I felt furious.

As pissed as I'd ever fucking been in my life.

Cam wasn't my family. He wasn't my friend.

He was just a guy I'd grown up with. A neighbor.

Surprise is slick. It'll snap your fucking nose.

I stepped outside before Mae spotted me. I'd stopped smoking cigarettes, but I grabbed her pack on the bench anyway. And I promised myself right there that I wouldn't think about Cam anymore, because he really had moved on, and whatever his life was now had absolutely nothing to do with me.

I pulled that off for a while.

35.

I've been asleep in my bedroom for twelve fucking seconds before Cam's peering over me, breathing in my face.

He's dressed for work. I'm extremely not.

I say, You could've knocked.

I did, says Cam. We can't find the extra hand mixer. Are you hungover?

No, I say. Fuck. I don't know. Why do you care?

I don't. But you stink.

It's three in the morning.

That used to be my excuse, too.

I blink myself awake while Cam smirks.

Did you have fun, he says. On your—

It was fine, I say.

That's good.

Are you being funny?

I literally gave the most basic compliment.

Maybe I'm just not used to that from you, I say.

Do you want me to be a shithead, asks Cam. Would that be better for you?

The look he gives me is genuine.

No, I say.

Cam looks like he's going to add something. But he simply raises his arms, stretching toward the ceiling.

Ivan's coming in late today, he says. His nephews are visiting from Mexico. And Noel doesn't know where anything is yet—

Who the fuck is Noel, I ask.

Cam shakes his head at this, running a hand through his twists.

Our new hire, says Cam. We did interviews over the weekend. They started today.

What? Mae already —

You weren't here. Mae didn't think we'd find anyone better, and we all agreed on Noel.

We agreed? Are y'all the UN now? What fucking we?

Me and Fati. Ivan too.

But no one thought to fucking ask me, I say.

They did, says Cam. Fati insisted, actually. And I told everyone you'd be fine with it.

You *what*, I say.

I'm on my feet before I even realize it.

Cam only blinks back, taking me in.

I thought you had other things to deal with, says Cam. And you did.

That wasn't your call to make.

Was I wrong?

I stare up at Cam. He doesn't look away.

And then I do.

Predictable.

I plop back down, rolling into a pair of sweatpants huddled on the floor.

How the fuck would you even know what to look for, I ask.

I grew up with Jin, too, says Cam. Where's the mixer again?

I tell him, and Cam nods, stepping backward and out of the room. But he turns around before he shuts the door behind him.

They're cool, he says. Trust me.

Famous last fucking words, I say.

36.

I remember telling Cam about the first guy I'd fucked. He looked genuinely happy for me.

And then incredibly bored.

It was a few years before I knew what that meant. This thing about me that I'd held so dear was as unremarkable as a fart.

37.

The first thing Noel asks is whether I need a glass of water. They're nearly a full head shorter than me. Smaller too. Tattoos cover one of their forearms. Pockets of hair tuft out from their cap, sitting below their ears, and their voice never rises too far above the music, and when Cam jokes about sticky palms, Noel smiles like they're about to laugh but they don't.

Noel wraps twelve kolaches in two minutes. They knead two bowls of biscuit dough in ten. They prep the butter cake batter and the banana bread and the scones. When Cam asks Noel for more flour, and an egg, and also a saucer and a spoon, they find these things wordlessly, immediately, stopping whatever they're doing on the other side of the kitchen.

Then Noel's right in front of me.

That's when I realize I've been staring.

You thirsty, they ask.

What, I say.

Like, for water? I'm grabbing one for myself, too?

Oh, I say. I'm good.

Right, says Noel. Cam said something about that.

Something about what?

That you're the captain of this ship, says Noel, smiling.

I'm a worker bee just like you, I say. No authority whatsoever.

Well, says Noel.

They extend their hand for a fist bump. I try not to get flour all over it, but Noel only grins.

I ask if they've worked at another bakery, and they nod.

Out in Oakland, says Noel. You ever been?

Not even once.

My aunt owned a coffee shop. Mostly old Chinese clientele. I helped out during the week, but we were never as busy as here.

And what brought you all the way to Houston?

Family, says Noel, and their tone puts that thread to an end.

A beat passes.

I'm sure that one of us should say something.

But I don't know what to say.

Noel just keeps smiling, perfectly content with the silence.

From the corner of my eye, I see Cam leering.

We're happy to have you here now, I say, reaching for a bowl, but that's when Ivan grabs my wrist, shaking his head.

Nice of you to show up, I say.

Tranquilo, says Ivan. The boys wanted some sweets.

But it's your day off, he adds. You're supposed to be sick and we're still in a pandemic.

What? I'm fine.

Not according to your mother.

You don't have to deliver her messages, I say. That's not your job.

But *you* work for Mae, says Ivan. So go be sick.

I turn to Cam, but he's throwing his shoulders into a mound of dough. And Noel's already beating eggs on the other side of the kitchen.

So I take off my apron. Turn to my phone.

There's nothing there but I stare anyway.

38.

When I prod Mae about Noel, she looks at me for a long time.

I don't see the problem, she says. If anything, they're overqualified.

I didn't say they weren't. I just wish you would've asked me.

I most certainly did.

You asked *Cam*.

And he asked you, says Mae.

Or he said he did, she adds, smiling.

We're on the patio. Mae's sipping coffee, pulling on a cigarette. I'm vaping on the steps beside her. At some point, we decided that smoking around each other was the least of our worries.

A shriek from the neighborhood breaks the silence between us. It's followed by a scattering of voices. They all sound white.

Noel's a good kid, says Mae.

They seem fine, I say. I just think you should've run this by me.

Which part, specifically?

Everything.

At this, Mae turns my way. She ashes one cigarette, yanking another from her pack.

TJ, she says. Is this really what you want to be doing?

What does that mean, I say.

This. The bakery. It's hard work, and—

I'm here, aren't I?

I know how much you care about this place, says Mae. And I know, even if you don't admit it, that a part of why you've stayed is for me. And I appreciate you, TJ—

That's generous, I say.

Generous of *you*, says Mae. It's your life. We only get one. But sometimes I wonder if being here is what you really want.

Then why haven't you asked me before?

Would you have answered honestly?

The screaming behind us escalates into laughter. Some whitegirls skip by the porch, hunched over red Solo cups. When they wave our way, Mae and I nod back.

You don't have to stay for Jin, says Mae. Even if you think that you do.

You don't think I fucking know that, I say.

Mae's eyes soften, and she smiles. It's enough to make me look at my feet.

The whitegirls pass by our porch again. They're obviously lost. Wasted and laughing even harder.

Your father loved this place, says Mae, but he's been dead for a while now. Even if it's hard, you have to live for yourself. What do *you* want?

I don't even know how we got here, I say, standing.

I've been meaning to say this for a while, says Mae.

Fine, I say. You said it.

And it's good that you hired Noel, I say. Everyone seems to like them.

Cam thought you'd say that, says Mae.

So now we're talking about him?

That depends. How do you think he's holding up, by the way?

Seems normal enough.

Try again.

I look at Mae. She studies my face, pressing her lips together.

I don't know, I say. It's harder talking to him now. And I don't think he wants to.

Of course he does, says Mae.

We haven't said anything that matters since he's been back from rehab.

It all matters. It all adds up. Just keep trying.

Yeah, I say. How long do you think he'll be here?

Mae cocks her head. I throw up my hands.

I'm not asking because there's a problem, I say.

Good, says Mae. He'd do the same for you.

But he didn't when he had the chance, I say.

Some smoke escapes Mae's nostrils. And the gaggle of whitewomen cross through our yard once again, hovering in front of the sidewalk.

One of them glances my way. Her friends have turned frantic, arguing.

You and Cam are more alike than you think, says Mae. Too alike, even. Make him feel welcome and he'll feel welcome.

He doesn't make it easy, I say.

Neither do you, says Mae. But all we have is each other.

And finally, one of the whitegirls approaches our patio. Mae winks at me before she waves her over, asking where exactly she and her friends are trying to go.

39.

Turns out everyone was right out about Noel: between the five of us, our orders fly through the door.

And also, they speak Spanish.

When I ask how that's possible, Noel just shrugs.

Thai mom, says Noel. Malaysian dad. But blame my aunt for the cooking, and the Spanish. She taught me everything I know.

Can we hire her too, I ask.

Noel laughs, shaking their head, dipping back into the batter.

40.

A month passes this way. We've never moved orders so quickly. A few local magazines have spoken to Mae, and it's always a whitewoman dressed in Heights chic.

Fati compiles the profiles and videos, posting everything on social. When I lean over her shoulder, she snaps her fingers in my face.

How about this one, she asks.

It's fine, I say.

Be specific. On a scale of ten.

Three.

Ten is *good*, TJ.

Shit, seven.

What the fuck? Are you okay? You still horny for Ian?

Fati turns away from her screen, looking up at me.

No, I say.

Really?

That's over. Fuck him.

Good, says Fati. But you should still give yourself a minute to feel.

Feel what?

I don't know. Whatever you've got to process.

I was a fucking side piece that got pushed to the side, I say. For years. That's it.

Give yourself a break, says Fati. That's just one part of it. You said so yourself.

I was wrong, I say.

Maybe, says Fati. But it's still how you felt.

We both hunch over another video. Mae's beaming into the camera. She thanks her team, and her community, and she makes sure to mention Jin.

41.

One morning I'm watching Noel knead when Cam nudges me. He asks if I can pass him a spatula.

We're almost like a proper business, he says.

So you think we were fucking around before this, I ask.

Not at all, says Cam, but his grin undercuts it.

42.

A few weeks later, Mae tells the team that we've never made more cash in a quarter. We're huddled in the kitchen, and she insists on opening wine to deliver the news.

Noel smiles. Cam claps. Ivan calls it a miracle.

When Fati asks if this means we're expanding, Mae says there's a long way to go before we even think about something like that—the lack of zoning, apparently, makes finding new buildings impossible. But she looks in the exact opposite direction of me.

Which is when, entirely out of nowhere, I feel fucking nauseous.

While everyone else chats, I dip outside toward the patio. And I'm reaching for my weed pen but of course I've left it inside.

So I just sit on the steps. The air's stuffed with humidity. Every breath feels like *work*, but somehow it's comforting that everyone else in Houston is dealing with this, too.

When the door opens behind me, I expect Fati looking to drag me back inside. Or Cam with my pot.

But it's Noel.

They hand me a mug, sipping from one of their own. Then they sit next to me.

Neither of us speaks. The mug's full of tea. Just down the road, we listen to a car's engine sputter.

Eventually I say, It's a little hot for matcha.

Ungrateful cunt, says Noel.

I nearly drop my fucking cup.

But Noel's just got this grin on their face, looking me in the eye.

It's disarming. I don't know what to do with that.

But it makes me smile, too.

That's when the car across from us finally starts. The guy behind the wheel pumps his fist. But there's a little girl in the back seat, and her expression doesn't change   if anything, she frowns even deeper.

43.

Ian calls the next morning. I don't fucking answer. I'm in the front of the bakery with Fati, talking to a whitelady who's convinced that she ordered a wedding cake from us. Her mask keeps sliding down her face, and this lady keeps jabbing at the fabric with one hand while her phone's in the other.

I know y'all have the order, she says. I confirmed.

I doubt that, ma'am, says Fati.

I *know* it. I have the receipt.

But we don't sell cakes, ma'am.

The wedding's *tonight*, says the lady.

Fati catches me glancing at my cell. When she sees Ian's name, she narrows her eyes.

You should take that in the back, she tells me.

This is a *disaster*, says the lady.

So I hide in the kitchen until my phone stops buzzing. When I look out the window, Cam's on the patio, laughing at something from Noel. They've both got greasy paper sacks in their hands. Probably cheeseburgers from up the road. And there's some kid standing with them, munching on his own sandwich. He seems like he's just barely in high school. I've seen him around the bakery.

Noel says something else, raising their hands. Cam nearly falls over, clutching his gut. The kid smiles with his teeth, covering his face, and my phone pings with voice mail and I play that shit immediately.

When Ian says *wedding invitation* ten seconds in, I trash the message.

A few seconds later, I realize what I've done.

When I try retrieving the file, it's already lost to the fucking cloud.

So I turn back to the window. Noel's gone. Cam's sitting beside the kid. He looks like he's explaining something, wearing a face I've never seen before. And the kid nods along, kicking the dirt. They stay that way for a while, crumpling paper bags in their fists.

44.

One afternoon, we're cleaning the kitchen when Noel asks Cam for a ride home to Bellaire.

Ivan just keeps mopping, ignoring the rest of us. Cam starts to speak, but then he stops himself.

Did I say something wrong, asks Noel.

No, I say. It's just that wonder boy doesn't drive.

Really, asks Noel. In this city?

Noel looks at Cam, who's still staring at me.

Well, says Noel. Maybe if Ivan's free—

I'll be here a while longer, says Ivan. I'm helping Mae with something.

Something, I say.

Tasks, says Ivan.

That makes me bite my lip. Ivan only smiles, shrugging.

I'll take you, I say.

No no no, says Noel. It's fine.

So you'll inconvenience everyone but me, I say.

That's not what I mean, says Noel.

Before they can protest anymore, I slip off my apron, swapping my sneakers for a pair of slides.

And it isn't much longer before Noel's in my car, slinging a backpack across their lap, pulling up the directions on my phone.

They don't say anything as we pull out of the Heights, swinging across 610 and its traffic. But I didn't put on any music when we started. So it feels fucking ridiculous to do that now.

When I turn to Noel, they're looking out the window. We're dressed nearly identically, in hoodies and running shorts.

How long have you been in Houston again, I say.

Ah, says Noel. Just a few months.

Lots of Californians are making their way south.

Yeah. But I moved back with my aunt. She wanted to be closer to her kids, and the Bay can be intense if you're older. Unless you're white.

So you've got other relatives around?

Just some cousins.

What do they do?

They're both surgeons.

Shit. So they're smart.

On paper. One's plastic, one's brain.

Ha. And did your parents stay in the Bay?

Nah, says Noel. Dad's back in KL. Mom's in LA.

Traffic creeps to a lull.

All of a sudden, I'm conscious of being too nosy.

But Noel turns toward me, folding their arms.

I miss the weather out west, says Noel. But Houston's nice. Calm. I'm just trying to get my aunt settled before I make any plans.

Traffic gradually unfucks itself. The cluster of smoke shops and payday loan sharks lining Alief start thinning out. Farther down the road, every business is plastered with Spanish, until every other street sign is sporting Chinese, until every other restaurant is advertising phở.

And how's that going, I say.

How's what going, says Noel.

Living with your aunt?

She's cool, says Noel. Very classy. Tech savvy.

All great qualities, I say.

I'm kidding.

Oh.

And then I don't know what to say at all.

But Noel seems to accept that, leaning their elbow against the window.

We pass a pair of Buddhist shrines and a flower shop before Noel points me toward an intersection. The houses are all pastel one-stories. When we pull in front of one home, it's surrounded by bushel after bushel of jasmine shrubs.

A lady sits on the front porch. She waves when I put the car in park.

But Noel doesn't get out.

And I don't say anything either.

Listen, says Noel, don't freak out.

I was fine until you said that, I say.

My aunt's not gonna let you leave without cooking for you, says Noel. If I send you off without offering, she'll be pissed.

You don't have to—

I actually do, says Noel. This is me making my life easier. That's all.

Noted.

So do you want to come inside?

Noel's already got one hand on the door. They look as earnest as I've ever seen them.

Why not, I say. Fuck it.

Good, says Noel. Just don't be weird.

I'm being weird?

Nah, says Noel. You're great.

Cool, I say.

But don't start, says Noel.

45.

The inside of Noel's house is both antique and modern. For every gilded photo frame, there's a portable speaker. For every potted plant, there's a slick cooking tool. Repurposed chili crisp and coffee tins cover the counter, and I park myself in the kitchen while Noel leads their aunt back inside.

They chat at each other in Thai. Noel's aunt talks and talks. Noel simply nods, humming, shrugging their shoulders.

When I glance up from my phone, the aunt's staring me in the eyes.

Mimi wants to know what your name is, says Noel.

Should I say something, I ask. Will she understand?

Your name is your name, says Noel.

So I tell her it's TJ.

Mimi cocks her head a little bit.

Then I tell her my Korean name, and she smiles, nodding.

She moves me to a tiny stool. I test it before committing my whole body to it. Then Mimi and Noel proceed to flit around the kitchen, pulling at pots and pans, moving in a relaxed way, but precisely, waving their arms wherever for this or that but somehow always finding it.

A few moments later, Noel sets a bowl of curry in front of me. It smells heavy on the fish sauce. When I take a sip, it's creamy, sweetened with coconut milk—and it's entirely fucking delicious.

Jesus shit, I say.

This makes Noel's aunt wince.

Sorry, I say.

Don't let her fool you, says Noel. Everyone loves her curry.

The pair stands across from me, watching me eat.

When I slow down, Mimi sighs.

When I speed up, she gives a little smile.

I watch Noel bite their cheek to keep from laughing.

So, I say, how are you liking the bakery?

Everyone's nice enough, says Noel. Ivan and Fati have helped me get settled. Cam too.

They're a good group, I say. Or at least Ivan and Fati are.

Is Cam your boyfriend, says Noel.

There's no change in their tone of voice. They lean on the counter, slipping out of their hoodie, smoothing out the Warriors jersey underneath it.

That's pretty forward, I say.

It affects me too, says Noel.

You know, working dynamics, they add quickly, and I spot the hint of a blush.

Mimi follows us with her eyes. Eventually, she sighs, turning to a soap playing in the next room.

Then you can rest easy, I say.

So you're just friends, says Noel.

We grew up together, I say.

That's really cool. That you've stayed in each other's lives.

It's something.

It's rare. I don't talk to anyone from when I was a kid. People just kind of disappear.

Well now you're a part of our thing, too.

Noel blushes even further.

I start to clarify, but I don't know what the fuck I'd be clarifying.

So we're silent for another moment. I eat while Noel watches me eat. Mimi burps from the living room, and a laugh track chuckles beside her.

Cam's a good friend then, says Noel. He really cares about you.

When your rent is free it's the least you can do, I say.

But most people only get one or two folks like that their whole lives.

Are you saying you're jealous, I ask.

Noel opens their mouth, and then they close it. They turn their back on me, walking toward the stove.

Just like that, I've pushed too far.

Sorry, I say. I mean—

I know what you meant, says Noel, fishing through cabinets.

They pull out a bowl, ladling some curry for themselves. Then they settle across from me, still red in the face, until the two of us are *both* blushing. Looking like a pair of idiots.

Ah, I say. So there's something you should probably know about Cam. And his not driving.

I was wondering about that, says Noel.

Yeah. He was in a bad situation, back when he lived in LA. His boyfriend was killed in a traffic stop.

What?

By a cop, yeah.

What, says Noel, and they look me in the eyes, sitting up.

Cam's managing now, I say. Or I think he is. I don't know. You probably don't ever really get away from something like that? But it was in the news for a while, and Cam had to deal with that, and the court sided with the cop pretty quickly. He said he felt threatened, and they bought that. So he ended up with a suspension, for a bit, but he appealed it, and—

Fuck, says Noel.

Yeah, I say. So, you know, that's how that turned out. It's fucked. But Cam's coping, I think, in his own way. And he used to live with my family when we were in high school. So he's got, like, a familiar environment. But it's still a lot. Even if he doesn't say it.

I can't even imagine.

Neither can I. But he's here.

Okay, says Noel. Shit. Thanks for sharing that. I never would've known.

You could probably ask Cam about it, says Noel, if you want to. He seems to like you.

Oh, says Noel.

Which is when Noel's aunt steps back in the kitchen. She says something in Thai. It sounds like a question. Noel waves it away, responding just as quickly, then Mimi laughs, setting a hand on my shoulder before she leaves again.

I start to ask Noel what she said.

But I change my mind.

And then I'm done with my curry.

And since there's no reason for me to stay any longer, Noel walks me back outside.

The block is balmy. Cars are littered all over the curb. A few porches down, a Black family guffaws about something on a bunch of lawn chairs. When they wave at the two of us, Noel and I wave back.

Then Noel asks if I know how to get home.

I'll find my way, I say.

Don't get lost, says Noel.

And you're a good eater, says Noel. That's what my aunt said.

Is that a compliment, I ask.

It's an observation.

Then I'll take it.

And a good friend, too, says Noel.

Before I can say anything, they tap the hood of my car, walking back up their patio and shutting the screen door behind them.

46.

That night, Ian leaves another voice message.

I let it sit in my inbox for exactly three hours.

Then it's a little past midnight when I finally press play.

The neighborhood's quiet for once. Cam's watching *Anaconda* in the game room. Jennifer Lopez's warnings waft down from the hallway.

Hey, says Ian. Just calling to see how you're doing.

He adds: You don't have to call back.

His voice is soft. He pauses every few seconds. When Ian exhales, I hear footsteps in the background. And a woman's voice.

There's a pause on the line like he's about to say something else. I can nearly see the face he's making. But that's when his message ends.

An automated voice asks if I want to delete it, replay it, or leave my own reply.

So I listen to it again.

And then again.

And then again.

I don't mean to touch myself but that's what ends up happening.

Just as I'm close, when I'm starting to really *feel* him, I hit repeat for a tenth time and there's a knock on the door and of course it's fucking Cam.

I wait a beat to see if he takes the hint.

But he knocks again.

And I waddle to the door, cracking it open.

Cam raises an eyebrow from the other side. He's holding Mochi under his elbow, and the cat looks fucking annoyed.

You're flush, he says.

What the fuck do you *want*, I say.

Should I come back?

You're already here.

But are you busy?

I'm here talking to you.

Cam gives me a long look. He's grown out his facial hair the last few weeks. And his clothes are loose; he's in a sweater and my basketball shorts, but he's clearly gained weight. Back when he started eating with Mae and me, I didn't think much of it. Then I realized it'd been years since I'd seen Cam finish a meal. Let alone sit at a table for more than a few minutes.

And he just blinks at me now.

Cam says, I asked if you've got any toothpaste.

Sorry, I say, and I stumble toward my bathroom, handing him a tube.

Cam takes it. But he doesn't move.

Can I literally do anything else for you, I say.

No, says Cam. Good night.

Right.

Sleep tight.

Goodbye, Cam.

I wait until he finally turns his back, loping down the hall with Mochi.

And I pick up my phone, trying again.

But the moment's gone.

So I toss it onto a pillow instead, groaning into the mattress.

47.

A week later, Mae calls us in for a meeting before work. The five of us settle around her in the kitchen. When Fati looks my way, all I can do is shrug—I never got a heads-up.

But Mae's news is simple: There's been interest in our property from realtors in the neighborhood.

They've seen that we're doing all right for ourselves, says Mae. Everyone knows this place sees a lot of traffic.

But I'm not interested in selling, she adds. So if anyone drops by, you can tell them as much.

Cam nods, chewing his gums. Ivan and Fati stay silent. Noel keeps their eyes on Mae, until they meet mine, and we both look away.

That's all, says Mae.

You mean we aren't putting it to a vote, I say.

Everyone turns to me. Mae doesn't even flinch.

I already did, says Mae. It was a vote of one.

Ivan whistles, laughing. Fati shakes her head. They both clear out of the room, and Noel grimaces as they head toward the register.

Which leaves Cam and me with Mae.

You could've mentioned this earlier, I say.

It's a recent development, says Mae.

I mean to *me*, I say. Personally. Because I live here, too.

I know, says Mae. And you're right.

Do you plan on selling eventually, says Cam.

Shit no, I say. She has no reason to.

But Mae doesn't say anything to that. She just looks at Cam, and then me.

This place belongs to you both, too, she says. We didn't make a home just to give it away.

Just barely, I feel Cam exhale beside me.

So you're really saying that they haven't reached your price yet, I say.

Not quite, smiles Mae. But if they do, I might let you know.

48.

A few days later, some whiteboy from an app asks me to drive out to Richmond.

We've been talking for a few weeks. His photos are cute, in a neighbor-you-wouldn't-mind-getting-plowed-by kind of way. When I tell him I can't host, he offers up his place, but the suburb sits a little over an hour outside the city.

I've only fucked a few other guys since the trip with Ian. Which was months ago. And it's not like I haven't had other options. If Cam taught me nothing else, it's that someone's always down if you know where to look. But whenever I message anyone outside of my usuals from the bathhouse, finally working up the nerve to actually *meet* them, something always comes up.

I'll send the guy a dick pic, after he asks, and I'll never hear from him again.

Or I'll find out that he isn't into fucking Black guys.

Or that he isn't into fucking Asian guys.

Or that he's *only* into fucking Black guys if they top him, or *only* into fucking Asian guys if they bottom.

But while I'm packing a gym bag for the night, Cam watches me from the game room sofa. He doesn't say shit while I pull on my socks. When I step outside, Cam stalls in the doorway. And just as I start to lock up, he blocks the door with his foot. Mochi peeks his head through the crevice, purring.

Isn't it a little late to be driving, he says.

I'm a big boy, I say.

Well, says Cam. Just don't get pulled over.

He looks mournful when he says it. I wonder if I should hug him. But then Cam shuts the door in my fucking face, and that's what I'm left with as I creep onto the highway.

49.

If you drive west on I-10 late enough at night, you'll join the trickle of eighteen-wheelers and highway cleaners and the club set and the road trippers and all the other stragglers zooming into the darkness. It's pitch-black except for our blinkers. We're flanked by neon church billboards and insurance signs. But when I pull onto the feeder road, my surroundings flatten into Targets and Starbucks and too-bright football fields.

I message the whiteboy at a stoplight, letting him know that I'm close. He pings back immediately about how he's excited to see me. Then I ask for his apartment number, and I don't get a response, and I pull into the cul-de-sac before I try him again.

Of course he's already read it.

But he hasn't reached back.

So I send him another message, waiting a beat, and he doesn't respond to that either.

At the very least, I'm not stupid enough to park in a white neighborhood overnight. So I end up settling into a nearby school's parking lot.

I check my messages again.

The whiteboy's online, but he still hasn't reached back.

A cop car drifts through the lot, so I drive until I find somewhere emptier.

I end up at a park by the lake. Some Latinx teens smoke on the swings. They're living their own high school romance, watching TikTok on a phone shared between them.

When you realize you've been ghosted, it doesn't even feel like an epiphany. There's just this funny feeling that starts in one corner of your head. Then it seeps into your gut. It climbs down your spine until it ends up in your toes.

So I turn off my car.

And my lights, too.

The teens across from me laugh, and that drifts in through my windows.

50.

I'm not sure when I fall asleep, but when I jolt up it's just past four. The teens are gone. I never heard back from the whiteboy. But a few other guys sit in my inbox, selling meth and Cialis prescriptions.

And then there's a text from Cam.

U ok?

👍

Good. Bring back food

I start messaging Cam to go back to sleep. But before I can talk myself out of it, I text Ian instead.

It's just a few words.

Hey. Hope you're good.

Then I put my cell down, closing my eyes for a little longer. I'm glad I saw a Whataburger flashing by the exit, because that's the only thing keeping this from being a fucking bust. I might as well pick something up for Cam, too.

51.

Some days, Jin took me on drives across Houston. This was one of his great joys. When he'd first arrived in Texas, its drivers appalled him, until he finally became one and all of that resentment disappeared.

His first car was a used blue Jeep. He sold that for a Corolla. Then he sold *that* one for a pickup truck, and he liked lying in the back of it, hiding away from Mae as if she didn't know where he was.

The three of us drove to just about every park in the city—it was the one routine in our lives that we kept separate from Cam. I have no idea what he did after we'd leave, waving as our car drifted away from the front porch. But Jin and Mae usually packed some kind of lunch: kimbap and ham sandwiches and Tupperwares of kimchi and burritos from the taquería behind our house. I couldn't stand these outings at the time—they felt too fucking tedious. But Jin only laughed when he saw my face. He said that when I got older, quieter things would make me happy.

You'll see, he said, and he'd run his hand through my hair.

52.

A few weeks later, Noel tells me they need a favor.

Jesus, I say. Is this gonna get me in trouble?

Only if you say no, says Noel.

We're prepping in the bakery. It's just past five in the morning. Ivan's called out sick for his nephew's recital, and Cam won't make it into the kitchen until after his therapy session.

Mornings used to feel meditative, and Noel's being around doesn't change that too much. They work silently, floating across the kitchen. Every now and again, they'll glance my way with an exaggerated grimace.

My cousins are coming over for dinner, says Noel.

The surgeons.

Yeah. They want to check on my aunt.

The help must be nice, I say.

Please, says Noel. They're only lining up for a spot in her will.

I look at Noel until they turn their eyes to me.

Sorry, says Noel. You aren't trying to hear about my bullshit.

There are bigger things to apologize for, I say. It's hardly global warming.

The thing is, says Noel, Mimi wants to cook for them. She wants to show her kids a nice evening. She doesn't see that they're leeching.

Or maybe she does, I say, and the fact that they're her children is more important to her.

This is enough for Noel to stop kneading.

Are you always this wise, they ask.

Only with other people's shit, I say.

And it's sweet of you to help your aunt, I add. I'm sure she appreciates it.

Which is where the favor comes in, says Noel. We need help cooking the meal.

Oh, I say.

That *is* a favor, I say.

You can say no, says Noel.

Are you sure I'd be the person to do this?

I literally have no one else to ask, says Noel. Cam says he's busy—

He isn't fucking busy.

Yeah. Well. But if you don't think it's cool, then—

It's cool, I say.

Noel blinks at me a few times. Then they start kneading again.

You're sure, asks Noel. You're not just saying that?

Consider it done, I say. Happy to help.

Noel continues to knead.

Then they set a hand on my elbow, squeezing.

And we stand like that, for a moment, before something clatters and we both leap. But it's just Fati making her way into the building, yelling about how needlessly heavy the door is.

53.

When I tell Cam about Noel's dinner, he looks up from his phone. He's laid out on my bedroom carpet. I'm looking down at him from the mattress.

At some point, we fell back into this teenage routine. It happened wordlessly. And I didn't mind. Some days, after we close up shop, I'll spot him roaming around the house or dozing on the back porch. But my room is one of the few places that I've seen him so comfortable.

Are you asking for advice, says Cam.

I'm telling you a thing that's happening in my life, I say.

So you're asking for permission?

If that's what you want to call it.

Then honestly, he says, I think you should go.

I don't know, I say. That's pretty intimate.

It means Noel trusts you. That's pretty rad.

What's there to trust? This isn't a date.

Of *course* it's a date, says Cam, groaning.

He rolls onto his elbow, pulling at his cheek. I reach for his hand, stopping him.

They told me it wasn't, I say. Noel said it was just something they need help with. That's it.

Cam simply stares at me.

Noel told me they asked *you* first, I say. They told me you were busy. You lied.

No one lied, says Cam. Maybe I omitted some details.

I throw a pillow at his face. Cam catches it, sliding it under his belly.

Listen, he says. You're going to end up doing whatever you want to do. So if you don't want to go, then don't. Be comfortable. And you can daydream about what would've happened for the next fifteen years.

Cam says all of this in an even tone.

Then he turns back to his phone.

I don't have anything to wear, I say. I don't even have a fucking jacket.

You can borrow something of mine, says Cam.

How the fuck would I fit in yours, I say.

Then wear Kai's, says Cam. I still have a few things of his. You can look through them.

It's the first time that Cam's mentioned him all year.

I wait a beat to see if anything happens.

Is there something in my fucking eye, says Cam.

No, I say. Thank you.

Anyway, says Cam. If it really isn't a date, then why are you worried about what to wear?

54.

I don't fucking mean to show up late but I do and everyone's clogged at the door. Somehow we've all arrived at almost the exact same time. Noel's cousin Will wears a tie and loafers. Will's sister Emi rocks this glossy bodysuit under a leather jacket. And when I spot Noel behind them, they've tied most of their hair in a tiny topknot, wearing a button-down and khakis. It's the first time I've seen them so put together.

Meanwhile, I've pulled up in joggers and a Rockets tee and one of Kai's bomber jackets.

Noel's aunt waves. The cousins look at me like I'm a fucking dog. I smile at everyone, ducking into the kitchen, and Noel follows behind me.

Fuck, I say.

You're fine, says Noel.

I look like a fucking slob.

You're *fine*.

And you showed up, Noel adds. I wasn't sure.

I told you I would, I say.

People say a lot of things, says Noel.

When Mimi steps into the kitchen, she's wearing a pearl-blue dress that ends at her calves. It's kind of a showstopper. And she sets a palm on my elbow, the same way she did when we met.

She and Noel chatter in Thai for a while before it dawns on me, like a dumbass, that the three of us have work to do.

Mimi's motions are deft. Her knife skills are fluid. She shifts from pot to pan to prepped bowl to pan to pot and back. She talks at Noel, who translates for me, and every once in a while Mimi simply shakes her head.

We cook a whole fried fish, a shrimp stew, beef rendang, steamed cabbage, roti, rice, and stir-fried turnip cakes. It's an opulent spread. Easily enough for a family of ten.

And this is just for y'all, I ask.

Us, says Noel. You're eating, too.

No way.

You seriously thought I'd ask for your help without inviting you to our table?

When I ask Noel if we should add any dessert, they blink at me. And then they ask Mimi.

She replies in Thai.

Noel shakes their head.

Mimi simply repeats herself, ducking out of the kitchen.

She wants to know if you're down to cook something sweet, says Noel. But I told her that's too much work.

It's no bother, I say.

I don't even think we have—

You do, I say. I checked.

I say, Just let me do this. Go be with your family.

Noel really considers me. They chew on their lip, leaning on the counter.

Thank you, says Noel.

It's nothing, I say.

Before Noel can reply to that, Mimi calls them from the living room.

But Noel does a funny thing: they lean toward me, kissing me on the cheek.

Then they duck out of the kitchen.

When they open the door, there's a blast of Thai.

I look at the milk and eggs and sugar in front of me.

I think about something Cam told me once, that you really do bring your shit wherever you go.

55.

There's another memory that I can't shake: after Jin caught me with Cam, he started working longer hours.

I hardly ever saw him. He was working, or he was asleep, or he was simply "out." And I was too young to notice any shift in his relationship with Mae—as far as I knew, they were still warm toward each other. Still touching in the hallways and kissing as we started our mornings.

But one day, I asked Mae if something had happened. If Jin had told her anything.

We were cleaning in the kitchen. Jin was at the dealership—he still worked two gigs back then. Mae gave me a long look—and now I know that she was deciding what to tell me.

Are you worried about anything in particular, she asked.

No, I said. Things have just been weird lately.

Lately, said Mae, laughing.

More than usual, I said.

Maybe I should be asking *you* if anything's happened, said Mae. You know you can tell me anything, right? And that it'll be fine? No matter what it is?

But this was the thing: I didn't *want* to tell her anything.

I didn't want to explain or justify.

I didn't want to be *accepted* or *tolerated*.

I wanted to just be.

That's all.

Then she set a hand on my arm.

So I didn't bring it up again.

56.

When the yelling starts, I've just set a pot of tapioca pudding on the stove.

Will's voice booms out first.

Then I hear Noel's.

Mimi undercuts it quietly.

Then all three speakers rise against one another, until someone starts banging on the table, and Mimi has just started crying when I open the back door to smoke.

The night's balmy. Ranchero music plays in the next backyard over. A cheer rings out, with clapping and laughing, and that's when Cam texts me wondering if I can pick up tacos while I'm out.

It might be a minute.

Where are you?

Noel's.

Cute. Be safe! Want me to text them about that thing you like?

Fuck you. Good night.

Then I pull up the message I sent Ian.

He never replied to it.

I start to message him again, but the oven timer screams, and I pop back into the kitchen instead.

Except someone's already in there: Emi's riffling through the fridge. She does this thoughtfully, silently, like she isn't actually looking for anything at all.

And she's a scary beautiful woman. Makes no sense that it makes me nervous, but it does. I knock on the counter, and Emi gives me a once-over, extracting a beer before she shuts the fridge's door.

Our mom told us Noel had a friend here, says Emi. Nice jacket.

Thanks, I say. I'm only helping out with the food. It's a favor.

Pretty big favor.

It's nothing. We work together. Noel just wanted a nice evening for y'all.

They certainly tried.

Emi twirls the Singha between her hands, opening one drawer and then another. I remember spotting a bottle opener, so I pass it her way. And she thanks me, smiling for the first time since we've met.

Noel's got it pretty hard, says Emi. You know?

I can only imagine, I say.

Sometimes, says Emi, we think we're doing the right thing because we're told it's the right thing. Or because it's for someone that we care about. Or it's for someone who's cared for us. But it isn't the thing that *we* need. Sometimes it even hurts us.

Emi takes a long sip from her beer. She stares at me like I should respond.

Maybe we can only do what we can, I say. And we try to hurt as few people as possible.

There's no way not to hurt anyone, says Emi. Even if you really try. You'll only end up burning yourself.

Sure, I say. But I think it's still worth trying.

That's cute, says Emi. I can see why Noel likes you.

Is this about them, I ask. The yelling?

Emi takes another, longer, swig. And she smiles.

Not all of it, she says. I'm sorry, I'm intruding now—

You aren't, I say. Really.

Then can you do me a favor, asks Emi. Like the one you're doing for Noel right now?

I nod, despite myself. Emi sets her beer on the counter.

Be good to them, she says. They don't have many people they can rely on.

Okay, I say.

You sound like you mean it.

Because I do. I'll do what I can.

That's all I'm asking, says Emi.

Before either of us can say anything else, the door beside us bursts open.

Will clatters into the kitchen. He's loosened his tie, rolled up his sleeves.

He looks at me, squinting. Then he turns to Emi.

So you finally found the alcohol, says Will.

I did, says Emi.

It only took you an hour.

There's enough for you, too.

With that, Emi passes me, winking and squeezing my elbow. Will grabs his own beer before he turns my way. But all he offers is a single nod, eyeing the pudding before he shuts the hallway door behind him.

57.

The weeks Jin spent ignoring me passed by like the rest: I still worked in the bakery. Jin still smiled at Cam, praising all of his efforts. I didn't understand it—Cam was very clearly the issue, but that didn't seem like a problem to anyone but me.

When I asked Cam about this, he only shrugged. We were on the back patio, naked except for our shorts. We hadn't stopped touching since we'd been caught, but something had changed. It had started happening less. When I'd asked Cam about that, he said it was nothing—but I'd begun to think it was because of the difference between our bodies.

Cam had never been fitter. I'd always been chubby. And now that the novelty of fucking had worn off, and he had other options, I wasn't nearly as appealing.

You're overthinking it, said Cam.

I don't think I am, I said.

Then Cam rolled toward me, running a finger up my groin until I moaned.

I'm not going anywhere, he said. You'll see.

58.

After Noel's cousins take off, the table's still full of dishes. I can tell who sat where by which ones haven't been touched. And Noel's still at the table, grunting when I sit beside them.

Right after Emi left the kitchen, another argument exploded in the dining room. Noel yelled. Mimi sobbed. Will slammed the door when he took off, and I heard Emi whispering to her mother before she finally left, too.

Noel runs a hand through their hair, unraveling the bun. Neither of us says anything. But I place a bowl of pudding between us, and it's another minute before they reach for it, stirring everything with their spoon.

Pretty thick, says Noel.

New kitchen, I say.

We work with what we have, says Noel.

Or at least we try to, I say. Emi's pretty cool.

Was that your big takeaway from the evening, says Noel.

They take a bite of their pudding, fiddling with the spoon.

Sorry, I say.

No, says Noel. It's not you. Just my fucking family. It's always something with them.

Their face turns flush. They take another spoonful of pudding. I fold my hands under the table.

Mimi's got an ex-husband in Katy, says Noel. They'd been talking about getting back together. So she wanted to try and make it work with him in Texas, but her kids know that means she might sell the house in California.

It's a nest egg for your cousins, I say.

Exactly, says Noel. The way housing is in the Bay, they figure they'll cash out when she passes. Realistically, that won't be too long from now. But if she sells the place, who knows where that money will go.

To you, I say. For sticking around.

I don't fucking want it, says Noel. She took me in when my parents split up. Didn't ask any fucking questions. Gave me a job, and that's a fortune by itself, and I'll stay with her as long as she wants me to. But her kids think they know what's better for her than she does.

Because they're *her* kids, I say.

That's the argument, says Noel.

Jin used to say something like that, I say. The old know the most but they're heeded the least.

Your dad sounds like a smart guy, says Noel.

He's a dead guy, I say.

Oh, says Noel.

Heart problems, I say. They run in the family.

The two of us drink at the table, kicking our legs against it.

But the silence doesn't feel so uncomfortable.

It's like we're only taking the time that we need.

Then we open our mouths simultaneously.

No, says Noel, you first.

I was just gonna ask what you have waiting for you back in Oakland, I say.

Are you asking if it's a person?

I'm asking what I'm asking.

Noel clicks their tongue. They tap their bottle against mine, clinking the rim.

A job, says Noel.

Yeah?

With computers, if you can believe it.

Breaking them down or putting them back together?

Something in between.

Sounds expensive, I say.

Less than you'd think, says Noel. The company says they'll give me as much time as I need. But I'm thinking I'll head back in the fall.

You'll miss our famous Texas seasons.

You can text me photos of the leaves.

Noel grins, sipping from their beer.

I mirror the gesture but it comes off clumsy.

And there was an ex of mine, says Noel. He still lives in Oakland. We'd been broken up for months, but it felt like I had to leave the city, just to get some air.

Yeah?

Yeah. Being in a new place has helped.

Can I ask what happened, I say, and Noel grins again.

He wanted to settle down, they say. Which, fine. But he also wanted monogamy, which is his right, and I didn't think that was for me. It led to a lot of shit between us. And he made me feel, like, *wrong* for wanting what I wanted. I was starting to get used to feeling bad, as if that was normal, and things weren't good for a while. So that's when I broke things off.

Damn, I say. Sorry.

It happened. It's over. We learned a lot from each other and I hope he's doing all right.

I don't think I'd ever want a fully monogamous relationship either, I say. If I had one.

Really?

Yeah. I just think, you know, sex is a pretty important part of my life. And being able to really explore what that means for me. There are so many people, and spaces, that mean a lot to me, and I wouldn't want to cut those out entirely.

Is that right, says Noel.

It is, I say. And also, like, growing up, there weren't a lot of people who wanted big guys? Or anyone who did? And don't even get me started on how fucked up people treat poz folks. So I think finding people who were open to my body, and all of me, generally, helped me a lot with being okay with myself.

Sure, says Noel. I get that.

Yeah, I say. So I'd want my partner to have pleasure in their life, in the way that's best for them. As long as we're talking about it, I think that's what's most important to me. I think that whenever I've felt love, or been in love, it's only lasted when there was mutual feeling. Whatever that looked like. And I don't know if it can survive if the feeling's repressed.

Love can be a lot of things though, says Noel. Right? It's pleasure, but it's also washing the dishes and sorting medication and folding the laundry. It's picking out what to eat for dinner three nights in a row, even if you don't want to. And it's knowing when to speak up, and when to stay quiet, and when, I think, to move on. But also when to fight for it.

But I don't know what the fuck I'm talking about half the time, they say. So take that with two million grains of salt.

We both stare at each other. And then through each other. Noel takes another long sip of their drink.

I think that's probably the most I've talked in months, I say. Sorry.

Please don't apologize for being honest, TJ.

And what was *your* question, I say.

Why did you agree to help me today, says Noel.

The rest of Mimi's house shivers. A television murmurs down the hall. It sounds like a newscast from abroad, dipping in and out of commercials.

It's a little late for that, I say.

Now seems like the perfect time, says Noel.

I'm here because I want to be, I say. That's all.

Really?

Yeah.

Okay, says Noel.

What happens next feels natural: Noel rises from their seat, leaning across the table, settling in front of me until we kiss.

Then we kiss deeper.

Noel stands, placing their palms on my cheeks. They straddle me in the chair. I wrap my arms around their waist, balancing the two of us. I'm hard, and Noel grazes me, and when I squeeze their dick they're hard, too.

It's a few minutes before Noel looks up, alarmed.

Wait, Noel says. Is this okay?

Yeah, I say. Are you okay?

I'm good. Should we talk about STDs?

We can, I say. I'm poz undetectable. That's it.

Cool, says Noel. I'm not poz. Nothing else to add.

We stand, slipping our arms into each other's shirts.

Then we fumble into the hallway.

And then a bedroom, where Noel toes their door shut before settling me onto the mattress.

They've got a single print of some painted mountains on one wall. Some potted plants dot the windowsill of another. The wood creaks underneath us, and the air smells like incense, and I'm about to ask them about the scent when Noel sets their mouth on mine.

They take my shirt off, and I pull off theirs. I tug off my sweats and Noel pulls off their pants. I start reaching for Noel's boxers, and they reach for mine, and we're both on their mattress with our hands on each other's asses and that's when they take a breath.

Can I say something, says Noel.

Yeah, I say.

I don't know if I want to fuck you, says Noel. Not yet.

Okay, I say. Right.

Our bodies sink into the mattress. Noel leans onto their elbow.

All of a sudden, I feel entirely too exposed.

Wait, says Noel. Can I start over?

Please, I say.

I *want* to fuck you, says Noel. I've *wanted* to fuck you.

That's a significant revision, I say.

But I don't know if it's a good time, says Noel. I mean, you've seen this situation with my family. I don't know how much longer I'll be in Houston. And I like you, and I think I could really keep liking you. But I don't want to put you or me in a bad spot. I've rushed things before, and it's never turned out well.

I reach for a bedsheet, but it's a little too far from me. Noel hands it over.

Then I think about it.

I set it aside.

You don't have to explain yourself, I say.

Yeah?

Yeah, I say. I'm not into doing anything you don't want to do.

Noel's body immediately relaxes. They roll into me, until our chests are touching, and noses too.

Are you being an asshole, says Noel.

No, I say.

Really?

Really. You're good.

Cool. Then, on that note, I'm not really into penetrative sex either.

Yeah?

Yeah, says Noel. I mean, hand stuff is fine. Fingering and all that. But, you know, the fucking of it isn't my favorite thing. Maybe from time to time. But not always.

Okay, I say. Then what gets you off?

Generally? Eating ass, probably.

Eating ass is up there for me, too.

Noel looks at me for a beat longer. They run a hand through my hair.

But maybe we can just stay here tonight, they ask. Like this?

That sounds perfect, I say.

Okay, says Noel. Hey.

Yeah?

They give me a long look, and then they kiss me.

I can tell that Noel's thinking about whether to tell me something.

Never mind, says Noel, and they kiss me again, fondling my balls with their fingers, and when I wrap my hand around their dick, too, it's not long before we're both snoring.

59.

One day I was working in the bakery with Jin when I cut myself with a fucking bench scraper.

He was showing me how to fold croissants, taking his time with layer after layer. I thought I'd found a rhythm slicing the folds, easing the blade across each roll. Then I cut myself.

When Jin saw, he cradled my wrist. He held it as we walked down the hallway. He sat beside me on the sofa as he cleaned my palm, taking his time with the alcohol.

Did you tell Mom, I asked.

Jin looked at me for a moment. Then he started applying the bandage.

Tell her what, he said.

You know what, I said.

Maybe I do, said Jin. Maybe I don't. You'll have to be specific.

About what you saw, I said.

Every day of this life we see—

Fucking stop!

Jin kept pressing my hand. His movements were steady, but gentle.

That isn't my story to tell, said Jin.

But TJ, said Jin, listen. I need you to understand that you are my son. That's all that matters to me. I want you to feel however you need to feel, and to be the you that you are. Because I love you. If that's a part of you, then I love it, too.

Jin massaged my palm, molding his fingers alongside mine.

And I don't always understand, says Jin. But I want to. That's the only reason I'm sad. I'm sad I haven't shown you that you're safe with me, no matter what. Even if I don't know how to talk about these things. But I want to learn, and I want to watch you grow. That's the most important thing to me.

Okay.

Then I added, Thank you.

This was when Jin finally looked up at me, a little shocked. And I was, too. I wasn't sure what I'd thanked him for.

But Jin pressed the ends of the bandage against my palm, leaning into them. And that's how we stayed, until the sun dimmed in the window, and Mae called us both from the living room to ask what we were doing for dinner.

60.

When I wake up in Noel's bed the next morning, they're gone.

No texts.

No notes.

Their clothes are still on the mattress. And I'm still out of mine. So I pull on my joggers and head into the hallway. Mimi's sitting at the kitchen counter. She's got some murder podcast playing from the speaker, and she's yelling into the phone by her ear.

I nod, pointing toward the door, and she shakes her head rapidly.

I point at the door again, and she shakes even harder.

Instead, Mimi points to a pot on the stove, waving me over. Laughing into the phone, she pulls out a chair, pouring a bowl of congee for me, dropping scallions and fried shallots from above. Mimi stares at me until I finally sit down, and then until I've taken one bite, and then another.

Then she turns back to her call. She turns up her podcast. And Mimi laughs at whoever she's talking to, with her entire body, like she's just heard the funniest shit in the world.

61.

Noel doesn't show up to work the next day.

62.

Or the morning after that.

63.

Three days later, Noel calls in sick again. They won't be in for the rest of the week.

Fati gives me a long look after she tells me.

What, I say.

You know what, says Fati.

You think it's my fault?

I didn't until you said so, says Fati.

So I send Noel a text, asking if they're all right.

Perf, they write.

Just sick?

Just sick.

Anything I can do? 😇

Some bubbles appear from Noel's end. They disappear just as quickly.

And two minutes pass without a response, so I'm about to add something when the bakery door opens behind us: a messy-haired kid stands beside our shelf of pastries. A bouncy Korean track tinkles from his phone.

I've seen him around the building every few weeks. He's usually talking to Cam.

Can we help you, asks Fati.

Probably not, says the kid.

Cam's in the back, I say. Do you want me to grab him?

He knows I'm coming, says the kid. I'll wait.

Which leaves the three of us standing in silence.

Fati gives me a look, ducking away toward the kitchen. And the kid fingers the glass case housing our muffins and cookies, mumbling under his breath.

Then I recognize the song. It's by TWICE, from one of their early records.

So how do you know Cam, I ask, and the kid squints.

He used to live with us, says the kid. With me and my dads.

Yeah?

Yeah. And he's my friend.

It's nice of you to visit him, I say.

It's not like he ever comes to us, says the kid. We keep inviting him and he keeps putting it off.

The kid taps against the glass, singing under his breath. I quietly mirror his words. And that's when he looks up at me.

Are you Cam's boyfriend, he asks.

No, I say. We're just old friends.

That's what I thought. But I didn't know. He talks about you a lot.

And what does he say, I ask.

It's not bad stuff, says the kid. He just brings you up. And talks about, like, how you both used to live in this neighborhood. And how much it's changed.

Well, I say, he's right about that.

You should talk to him, says the kid.

What, I say.

Like about your feelings, says the kid. That's what Cam always tells me. Open up blah blah blah, you'll feel better blah blah blah, emotions blah blah blah bloop blah.

Funny. Cam should take his own adv—

I know. He's kind of a hypocrite? But I still think he's right.

The kid turns back to the pastry case, tapping against the glass.

He says, Once I started talking to, like, my dads, and my mom, and my friends, I started feeling better. About all sorts of things. I don't really know why. But Cam's the one who suggested it.

So you're like his disciple, I say.

And you're a comedian, says the kid.

He nods, turning back to the pastry case. And I reach inside it, pulling out an almond cookie, handing it to him from the register.

Thanks, he says. You're not like how I thought you'd be.

And how was that, I ask.

Taller. Are you a ONCE? Do you listen to NewJeans? Who's your bias?

Before I can answer, Cam steps out of the kitchen, placing a hand on my back.

So you've met Diego, he says. My tiny apprentice.

Looks like it, I say. Does he bake?

I would never work here, says Diego. But the cookie is good.

And Cam opens the door for the two of them, leading the way outside. But before Diego takes off, he turns my way, waving.

64.

Lately, Mae's been talking to more realtors.

She's gotten offers to expand Jin's. And she's gotten offers to leave the neighborhood. And she's gotten offers to off-load the bakery onto local investors.

One night after we've closed, Mae corners me in the living room. She says she's seriously considering selling. All I can do is blink at her.

Someone finally met your price, I say.

Nothing is final, says Mae.

Then why are you even telling me, I ask.

I just wanted you to know, says Mae. I said I'd tell you if things got to a certain point.

She stands with her arms crossed. I watch her from the table. Cam's lounging upstairs, and Mitski's voice drizzles from his speakers; a yawn from Mochi breezes down from above us.

What changed, I say.

The circumstances, says Mae. A lot of businesses are moving into the neighborhood. Some of them are looking to buy property outright. And the money would set us up for a long time, TJ.

But this place is *ours*, I say. You know?

I'm aware, says Mae.

I don't think you are. Because you can't put a price on that. On a home.

Are you out of your mind? Talking to me like this?

I'm the only one that *will* talk to you like this.

That's just not true, TJ.

It's close enough. And I'm the one who gets fucking burned. I'm the one who loses a home.

That isn't lost on me, says Mae. But is that really what you think?

What?

Homes can change, says Mae. Is this a home because you really believe that? Or because it's where you think you should be?

Is there a fucking difference, I ask.

I don't mean to raise my voice but it happens. The music from upstairs has gone silent. But Mae's expression doesn't change.

You wouldn't have to stay, she says.

Of course I would, I say.

But you wouldn't *have* to, says Mae. I've already asked Cam.

Mae has never struck me, but her words sit me down. The face she makes proves that she knew they would.

You've asked Cam about what, I say.

How he'd feel about making his arrangement a little more formal, says Mae. And a little more long-term.

I grimace. Shake my head.

I know I should be happy to hear this.

You can be angry, says Mae.

I'm not, I say.

Cam can do the work. It's what he knows. And he's able to do it nearly as well as you.

What did he say when you asked him?

Mae weighs the question. She chews her gums like she's considering what to tell me. I listen out for any noise upstairs, but if Cam's listening in then he's completely silent about it.

He asked if he could think about it, says Mae.

And you won't decide whether or not to sell until then?

That isn't how it works. But I'll take his decision into account, right along with yours.

Mae looks resolute.

It's how she was with Jin. They talked through everything together, but Mae was the one who made important decisions. From where to live, to the rhythms of our days, to when Jin would quit the dealership. Baking was the part of his life that he had complete control over.

So I stand.

And I say, Okay.

Okay what, says Mae.

It's fine, I say. Do whatever you want to do.

I'm thinking that she'll smile. Or acquiesce.

But Mae only frowns.

TJ, says Mae. I need you to be honest.

I *am* being fucking honest.

But with *yourself*, says Mae, and then she doesn't say anything else.

65.

When I find Cam, he's still lounging on my bedroom floor. Music's tinkling from his phone. If he heard us downstairs then he doesn't let on.

Hey, bard, he says.

Queen, I say. Is that Red Velvet?

Yeah, says Cam, "Bad Boy." You got me into them.

Look at you.

But hey, Cam adds. I think Noel lied about being sick.

You're a real Mare of Easttown, I say. An actual Inspector Koo.

Just doing my part, says Cam. You really haven't heard from them?

I know as much as you do.

Is your penis responsible for that?

Do you want to die?

I sit across from Cam. He wipes his nose.

It's another thing we used to do. Just sit across from each other. Sometimes we'd touch and sometimes we wouldn't, but we always had the proximity.

Is there something on my face, says Cam.

I need to ask you something, I say. But I don't know if I should.

Cam squints at me, scratching at his cheek.

It's Friday night, he says. Do you want to get fucked up?

What, I say.

I said do you want to go out and—

I fucking heard you, I say. Is that something you should be doing?

No, says Cam. The operative word was *you*.

I'll just babysit, says Cam. But maybe it'll help with your question.

66.

We don't go to a gay bar. Neither of us suggests it. Instead, we start at a taquería a few blocks from the house.

Tonight's crowd is mostly older Mexican dudes, with one table full of Black folks, and a handful of Indian kids running around the parking lot. The staff itself is almost entirely women. A Dynamo game drones on the television above us. Whenever the announcer raises his voice, we all look up. When his voice settles down again, everyone turns back to their food.

Our waitress pops chewing gum. She takes our orders, giving me a once-over. Dropping off our drinks and tortilla chips, she says something to Cam in Spanish and he laughs.

Is that your girlfriend, I ask.

Only on weekends, says Cam. She said you'd make a cute straight boy.

Fuck you, I say.

I'm sipping a beer. Cam stirs the straw in his water.

I've been coming here since I've been back in Houston, says Cam.

Any reason in particular?

The trade.

Seriously.

Cam cracks his neck. He runs his hand through his hair.

I have less context here, says Cam. Nobody fucking bothers me and there's no script. I'm not supposed to act or be a certain kind of way.

Did you feel that way in LA, I ask.

Sometimes, says Cam.

What about at the bar, I ask.

It's everywhere. The anxiety doesn't just go away.

And the bakery?

Cam doesn't say anything to this, chewing a handful of chips instead.

A hush falls over the room. On the soccer match, a Dynamo forward juggles the ball past another guy. He has a clear line to the goal but he trips over his own feet, clattering in the opposite direction.

Fuck, says Cam, I think there's a chip in my gums.

What, I say.

It hurts.

Then drink some water.

I finished it.

I'll order you another one.

Don't, says Cam. That's a sign. I want to go somewhere else. And don't try to finish that beer. You're driving, remember?

The shift is abrupt. Cam's shaky now, standing from the table.

So I shrug. Stand. When our server approaches the table, she turns from me to Cam. He smiles her way, setting a twenty on the table. And she nods, snapping the bill up instantly, effortlessly.

67.

Traffic on Highway 6 is fucked from the rain, but we end up at a Korean sauna in Spring.

I've never seen it before. Didn't even know we had one in Houston.

Years back, Jin packed Mae and me in a car for the jjimjilbang in Dallas. It was a seasonal thing. Jin scrubbed my back and I'd scrub his, then the three of us spent those nights huddled in the common area.

Jin called bathing one of the few joys in his life, laughing every time he said it.

And then, obviously, we stopped going.

Now a sleepy Korean dude by the door nods us inside. We drop our shoes in a locker, heading to the changing room, stripping at adjacent stalls before we find the bath. And there are only a few other men in the water: some Chinese guys, and a Japanese kid with his father.

Tinny jazz churns from the speakers above us. A clock looms over the bath, blinking. Sinking into the water, my whole body relaxes, and Cam rests his elbows on his knees, sighing.

How'd you even find this place, I say.

Google, says Cam.

Did the drugs make you this difficult to talk to?

You're the pot calling the fucking kettle black.

It's the first time I've seen Cam naked in years. His skin shines all over. He's got hair across his ass and his thighs and his calves. But he's mellowed out above his hips, and as we settle deeper into the bath, we groan.

Kai liked these places, says Cam.

Okay, I say.

He was always going whenever he could, says Cam. When we finally went together, I didn't fucking get it. And I still don't know if I do. But they remind me of him.

The bath's silent otherwise. Across from us, the Chinese guys whisper to each other. In the dry sauna behind us, a Black guy sits with a towel over his head, while two Latino men lie naked on their backs.

Cam sinks until the water barely skims his chin. I rest my elbows on the bath's edge. We spread our legs until our thighs just barely touch.

I wait to see if Cam moves.

But he doesn't.

So I don't either.

This is probably where I should say thanks, says Cam. For coming out tonight.

Because I was so busy, I say.

Yeah. Well. You could've been out with Jonah, from that restaurant.

He's just a friend.

Sure. And then there's Noel.

Ha.

Seriously. I really needed this, and you came through.

Cam rises from the water, just a bit. He drifts toward the pool's center, taking me in, blinking.

I backslid a bit, he says. Last night.

Okay, I say.

It wasn't much, says Cam. Or, you know, not as much as before I went to rehab. And therapy. When I'm struggling, my therapist has been helping me.

Sounds good, I say. And how's that going?

It's cool, says Cam. I'm working with Emma. This Nigerian lady. When I was in treatment, I'd talk about my situation, and the shit I was thinking, and sometimes it felt like people kind of cringed? And not even intentionally. Just that it was, like, too much for them? But no matter what I tell Emma, she doesn't even blink. And she says it's normal. Just me being a person.

Wow.

Yeah, says Cam. But anyways. I met up with these two guys last night and we fucked.

It's a human need, I say. You know how I feel about that.

Of course, says Cam. The sex was never the problem. I just let it get away from me. And I still have my regulars. The sober ones. They know about me and what I'm going through, and we've figured something out that works for everyone. But these other guys were new. It was my first time hooking up with them. And they had meth around.

Oh, I say.

Yeah, says Cam. They had it, you know, just to party. And I told them I couldn't do that anymore. So I left. But when I got back home, I took one of the pills I had left over from last year. Just to get back on level.

Right, I say. And how did that feel?

Great, says Cam. And then not so great. I didn't know what I'd do if I stayed in, and that scared me, but then you came around. So I asked if you wanted to hang. But, really, you're the one doing me a favor.

It's not a favor, I say. We're just out. It's nothing.

Fine, says Cam. But it means a lot to me.

He floats back toward the bench beside me, grazing my calf. After a moment, I set a hand on his thigh. And Cam flinches up, briefly, until his leg relaxes.

Thanks for telling me, I say. That must have been hard.

Yeah, says Cam. It would've been worse last year. But, you know, sharing is supposed to help.

I appreciate that you trusted me.

Don't sound so much like a textbook.

Fuck you.

That's better.

And, I say, I don't know if there's a better time to ask this, but has your eating been okay?

Yeah, says Cam. Therapy's been helping a lot with that. And having someone to talk to about, like, working with food? And how that feels a little fucked up sometimes?

Shit, I say. I had no idea.

Yeah, I mean, I didn't either. It was just a feeling. But now I think I'm getting a little better at putting those into words, or at least trying to. Instead of, like, trying to fix myself. Or be fixed. Which'll never happen. Or at least as long as I'm here.

Sure, I say. Work in progress.

Something like that. It's baby steps, and sometimes I don't know if I can do it. But it's still movement, I guess.

You're right, I say. It is.

Cam sets his hand on mine, squeezing. He holds my hand, and I hold his. I glance at the guys across from us, but they're lost in their own conversation.

You want to know something, says Cam.

You'd tell me even if I didn't, I say.

Sometimes I still see him, says Cam. I'll talk to Kai like he's right in front of me. I don't know why it started happening, but one day it did.

And it fucking scared the shit out of me, says Cam. In the beginning. That shit didn't even happen with my parents, and I'm only just starting to figure out how much that fucked me up. I didn't even let myself think about them. For years. When I finally did, what happened to them only made sense when I was high. But then one day Kai pops up, and he's just hanging out. Like nothing's changed. And now I'm terrified that it might stop happening.

Cam's hand relaxes. Mine does, too. One of the Chinese guys laughs, sending a ripple through the bath. His friend shushes him down, and when they look our way, we all nod.

What do you two talk about, I ask.

Nothing in particular, says Cam.

You get to chat with a dead guy and you've got nothing to ask him?

It isn't like that.

I don't know what I'd do if I saw Jin, I say. I spend my whole day trying not to think about him, and he still pops up in my head. Who knows what I'd actually say.

Jin died naturally though, says Cam.

Does that matter?

I think so. Because I'm the reason Kai's gone.

I don't say anything to that. I kick my feet out instead. My toes rise just above the water, creating their own tiny bubbles.

Kai would still be here if he hadn't met me, says Cam. And I don't know what to do with that. Like, he's the most important part of my fucking life, and he fucking changed me, and he'd have been better off if we'd never met.

Okay, I say.

But the two of you *did* meet, I say. It happened.

Two more Asian guys enter the water beside us, sinking into the center of the pool. One of them slaps the other's ass. His friend shoots him a look. When the thunder outside ripples, the lights flicker above us.

What would've happened isn't your business, I say. You can't worry about that. It'll kill you, too.

Is that right, says Cam.

I don't know if it's right. It just is.

Sounds like some shit Mae would say.

Because she did.

Cam turns to me then. Tucks his hands into his armpits.

When did you turn into a fucking therapist, he says.

I learned a little while you were away, I say.

The Black man from the dry sauna waddles toward us. He dips a toe into the bath before he settles into it, closing his eyes. When he grins our way, we both smile back—and then Cam taps my shoulder, so I rise beside him, dripping water all over the tile.

68.

We collapse onto a pair of futons. Other folks laze around us, tapping on their phones or whispering or doing their best to sleep. Two Korean teens lie a few futons away, sharing headphones plugged in a laptop and a bowl of peanuts. On another set of futons, a Black woman braids her daughter's hair. She takes care with every strand, while the girl cradles her mother's foot.

Cam covers his eyes. We're in the sauna's pastel uniforms, staring up at the ceiling. The rain's gotten softer but it still patters above us.

I haven't decided whether I'm staying yet, says Cam.

He's still got his hands on his face. I roll on my hip, facing him.

For years, after Cam left, I'd wanted to hurt him the way he'd hurt me.

The thought kept me up at night. I'd lie awake rehearsing my words.

And my chance has finally arrived.

If I tell Cam to leave, it will destroy him.

Saying nothing might be even worse.

Good, I say.

You should stay, I say, if that's what you want.

Cam opens his eyes. He rolls over, looking a little surprised.

Yeah?

Yeah. We'd figure something out.

And what about you, says Cam.

What about me?

What will you do?

What does that have to do with you, I ask.

Everything, says Cam. If I stay, then you can go.

Rain keeps falling above us. The room's lights dim.

I'm still circling around what to say when I feel the beginning of sleep.

But I jolt awake hard. Cam's snoring beside me. And the snores of everyone around us seep through the darkness, too.

Just beside our futons, the two teens on their laptop look up at me. The screen illuminates their faces. We're all a little surprised to see each other.

They both flash finger hearts. I send one back.

69.

A few days later, Noel's back in the bakery.

Just had to figure some things out, they say.

I thought you were sick, I say.

Eh. That too.

But now you're better?

More or less, says Noel. Isn't living a terminal condition?

70.

We spend most of the week revolving around each other. On a busy day, when Noel steps outside for their lunch, they ask if I want to join them.

We settle onto the patio. The weather's starting to turn. The air's balmy, and Houston's humidity has given us something like a truce.

That's when Noel reaches into their bag, handing me a paper sack of turnip cakes.

I asked Fati what you might like, says Noel.

This place has the longest line, I say.

I was in the area, says Noel.

Which is obviously a lie. It's nowhere near the Heights.

But I take a bite. It's delicious.

I hold the bag out for Noel to share. They give me a long look before they reach for a pair of wooden chopsticks.

71.

Mae wants to know if I've made up my mind.

It's fine if you haven't thought about it, she says.

It's *all* I think about, I say.

The two of us are wiping down the glass pastry cases. We've closed shop for the day.

I'm not rushing you, says Mae. But I've made a decision.

And what's that?

Mae crosses her arms. I dig my toes into the wood.

We're keeping the home, says Mae.

Okay, I say.

But we're still expanding, says Mae, and we'll be moving Jin's outside the house. I've already found the new building. It isn't far, but it's more space.

Great, I say.

You don't have anything else to add, asks Mae.

It sounds like you've made up your mind, I say. You and Cam have everything figured out.

Mae considers me for a moment. Then she shrugs.

But she doesn't add anything else. She'll wait for me.

72.

Every fall, our corner of the Heights throws a block party called White Linen Night. It's mostly drunk white people stumbling around in white T-shirts. Everyone stinks from the humidity. But everyone's smiling regardless, and most of the strip's businesses are open, and the bakery sells a week's worth of goods in an afternoon.

Afterward, we drink on the patio watching the foot traffic. Partiers pass, laughing too loudly and sweating all over one another.

And that's when Mae tells everyone else about the move. She grips the banister, beaming.

Ivan claps at the news. Fati just smiles. Tapping her cup against mine. Usman stands beside her, looking mellow and laughing at the two of us, then he kisses Fati on the cheek, disappearing into the crowd.

Your dude has the kindest eyes, I say.

Stop it, says Fati.

I'm just saying. I'd let him.

Then go fuck each other in a corner somewhere, says Fati. Just leave me out of it. But who was that guy who came by earlier?

Oh, I say. Jonah? He's a friend.

Just a friend.

Just a friend. He runs a restaurant out in Spring.

Mm. Well, he's cute. And you seem to have a lot more of those lately.

What?

Cute friends. It's clearing up your skin.

Thanks for nothing.

You're always welcome, says Fati. And you could pretend to look a little happier about the new space.

Sure, I say. It's just the end of the fucking world.

Don't be like that. It's a net win for all of us.

And Mae.

Especially your mom. You could try being happy for her.

She's doing a pretty good job of that on her own.

And you could try thinking about someone other than yourself. Maybe this will actually force you to make a decision.

When I ask Fati what she means, she only shrugs. But then Ivan begins a song, some kind of kitschy vaquero ballad, and Noel laughs along with him, linking elbows and looking my way.

Which is when I spot Cam. He's bullshitting with two other guys across the patio. And, before this, a bunch of queers had tracked him down in the yard, waving their hands and laughing. Cam looked familiar with all of them, patting their backs and slapping their shoulders. I had no idea how extensive his network was—all of these people had come for him. He was beloved, even if he didn't know it.

When Cam catches me staring, he waves me over, until they're all grinning my way, and it's the warmest I've seen Cam in the past few months.

TJ, says Cam, this is Minh. And that's Devon. Minh and I worked together in a past life and Devon is his boyfriend.

We haven't actually been using that word, says Minh.

He's joking, says Devon.

I'm really not, says Minh.

It's fine, says Devon.

And then Minh turns to me, opening his arms and wrapping me in a hug.

Oh, I say.

It's okay, says Minh. I'm drunk. And also you're famous!

Really?

Bitch, yes! Cam *loves* you! Has he told you that lately? I remember when you first started coming to Harry's.

Maybe we should get you a glass of water, says Devon.

I'm serious, says Minh. You're his best friend!

Doesn't he have work tomorrow, asks Cam.

Whatever, says Minh. I'll call in sick.

That's different for you, says Cam.

It's a new job, says Devon. Maybe save your sick days.

What do you do, I ask.

Speech pathology, says Minh. It's been a long time coming. And it's a lot of work. But it's how I met Dev. And I've really never been happier.

Enough, says Cam. Now you're being ridiculous. Maybe you can grab some ice for him, Devon?

Yeah, says Devon. It was nice meeting you, TJ.

Lovely meeting you, says Minh.

I'll catch up with y'all later, says Cam.

As his friends wave our way, Cam and I stand on the patio, leaning on the wood until they're out of sight. Then Cam shakes his head, standing and leaving the scene.

So I follow him inside—down the hall and onto the back patio.

He stands with his hands under his armpits. And we stare out at the backyard while the sounds of the Heights muddle around us.

Who would've thought we'd still be here, says Cam.

Not me, I say.

Fuck.

What?

Do you know how hard I fought to leave? And now look at my ass.

Is that a bad thing?

No, says Cam. It just is.

Well, I say, I'm still here, too.

Cam gives me a look. It's more mournful than anything I've seen from him in ages.

But that's when the door opens behind us. Ivan stands with a pair of beers and a soda.

What are we talking about, he says. Redlining? Homophobia? Is that why we're frowning?

Actually, we're celebrating, says Cam, brushing by me before I can stop him.

73.

We're closing up when Noel asks if I'd like to go for a walk with them. They say it matter-of-factly, like they're asking about the weather.

Unless, Noel adds, you're planning on dancing in the road like everyone else.

I say, I don't really do that.

Too bad. That'd really be something.

I guess we'll never know.

Fati and Usman have already taken off. Ivan and Mae have disappeared, too. And Cam is somewhere with his friends, which makes Noel and me the last two in the building—so I slip on a pair of slides, locking the bakery's door behind me.

Foot traffic's only picked up on the street. Noel and I look entirely out of place. The block's usual families have been replaced by boozy packs of white-boys and their girlfriends.

I didn't even know Houston had events like this, says Noel.

It's here if you're looking for it, I say.

But that's not really your thing?

Depends on the evening.

This one seems fine, says Noel.

The deeper we step into the neighborhood, the less people are milling around. Trees grow knottier, crowding together. Some have been rotting for generations. Others were just planted, spanning several lots. It's a microcosm of the city—the very old with the brand-fucking-new—which is enough to give you whiplash if you turn away for too long.

But that's when Noel slips their hand into mine.

We slow our walk, keeping eyes on the concrete.

And when it starts to rain, the water falls all at once, so we jog to Noel's car on the corner, shielding ourselves with our hands.

Droplets splatter across the windshield. We clatter into the back seat. Out of nowhere, the sky collapses into itself.

Hey, says Noel. Sorry about disappearing on you.

You don't need to apologize, I say.

I know. Still. I've been in shitty situations with guys before, and it kind of fucked me up, but that's not something to take out on you.

Nothing's changed for me, I say, and I start to add something else, but Noel's tugging my arm, lying across the back seat's cushion and planting their mouth on top of mine.

It's difficult making moves in a Hyundai Elantra. Without saying a word, Noel and I unfold ourselves across both seats. I hit my head on the roof, slipping off my shirt. Noel pulls off their shorts, knocking their elbow against the door. When I start sucking them off, Noel grasps at my hair, until they roll the two of us over and Noel grinds into my mouth from above.

I've managed to kick off my boxers, until they're by my ankles, and I start lowering Noel onto my lap when they shake their head, spreading my legs instead.

Is this fine, Noel asks.

I nod.

They stick a finger in me, and then two more, jerking themselves off as they press me into the door. Our pace is slow. Then steady. Then brisker, until we can barely catch our breath. And Noel tells me they're close, dipping until our noses touch—but I'm too busy coming to respond, and then they finish, too.

Afterward, we thump into opposite corners.

Between the humidity and the rain and the heat in the car, we're fucking disgusting.

But when I turn to Noel, they grin.

I also manage to do something with my face.

And then there's a knock on the door.

The two of us jump.

When I crack the passenger window, a handful of white women stand under an umbrella, peeking through the car's steam. One of them asks if we're their Lyft. And I don't mean to laugh, but I do—until my whole body starts shaking, and Noel laughs, too, rattling the seat belt as we cackle under the storm.

74.

Jin took me out of the country once. This was just before I finished high school. We'd flown to Seoul for a funeral and a birth: Jin's father had died, and his brother and his wife had a new baby. Mae and Cam stayed behind to look after the bakery.

When our plane landed at Incheon, Jin gripped tight to my elbow. We spent our first night at a hotel, and the next evening on a flight to Busan. Jin's brother met us at the airport, in shorts and a tank top, waving and talking at me in Korean so quickly that I couldn't keep up.

He asked me my name, and I said TJ. When my uncle's eyebrows rose, Jin jumped in with my Korean name. Then my uncle told me that I looked nothing like my father when he was my age, laughing, and Jin made a face I hadn't seen before—one that I never saw again.

After that, we rarely went a few moments without Jin touching my shoulder or running a hand through my hair.

75.

A week after White Linen Night, we're packing up for the afternoon and Fati's beside me at the register.

Cam's off for the day. He had therapy earlier, and now he's allegedly meeting a friend. When I asked who it is, he said he didn't owe me a diary of his life.

Right, I said. But you're okay?

I'd tell you if I wasn't, said Cam. Thanks though.

Should you tell me where I can find you? Just in case?

Only if you start telling me when you're sneaking off with Noel. And also your one thousand random hookups?

Which, fine.

So I ask Fati if we're going out for lunch.

Don't we sell food here, she says.

I tell her it's a good question, opening our fridge for the curry puffs Noel brought from home. There's no way I'll eat all of them. I figure we'll share. And I spot Noel back in the bakery, hunched over dough beside Ivan.

Then I'm stepping away from the fridge when I turn to Fati, who's got this look on her face like what the fuck.

So I look at the doorway.

And it's Ian.

Ian Ian.

He just stands there. In a T-shirt and jeans.

This guy asked for you, says Fati.

Okay, I say.

I drop my pastry on the register.

I walk to the other side of the counter.

I turn around, and Fati's staring, and Noel's poking their head out from the kitchen, but before Ian shuts the bakery door I'm already behind him.

When he unlocks his car on the corner, I'm in the passenger seat.

Then we're on the road, pulling out of the parking lot.

Then we're out of the neighborhood.

Then we're on the highway, headed south.

We're silent the entire time. Haven't said shit about anything.

It's one of the rare days when traffic is seamless. Cars fly by us, floating along the rim of our road's constellation.

I think about what I'm doing, but what comes up for me doesn't compute.

So I decide to stop thinking altogether.

When I turn to Ian, he's squeezing the steering wheel, clued in to the road.

I say, I should probably ask where we're going.

Out of town, says Ian.

Be specific, I say.

Galveston, says Ian.

I don't say anything to that. Ian speeds up, slipping into the center lane. The city gives way to whole stretches of nothing, which settle into dirt before the water rises below us.

It's my parents' place, says Ian.

Surely you didn't ask them.

No.

Then won't they be pissed?

I don't care.

You cared a lot—

That was a long time ago, says Ian. A lot has happened since then. Sam left.

My phone starts vibrating. I mute it. Regardless of who it is, I don't know what the fuck I'd say.

We slow down a beat. Sunlight beams across the car's windows.

Sorry to hear about your fiancée, I say.

Really, asks Ian.

He looks at me for the first time since we've gotten in the car. There's genuine curiosity on his face.

Yeah, I say. Really.

And that's enough for Ian to turn back toward the road.

Thank you for coming with me, he says.

Yeah, I say.

I know I'm not being fair.

Nothing's fair, I say.

Ian doesn't say anything to that. I don't know what he could possibly add.

The drive drones on. Billboards broadcasting Jesus and truck stops and strip clubs shine around us. But I tell myself that I won't fall asleep, no matter how familiar all of this is. And I don't.

76.

The home that Jin and I arrived at in Busan wasn't too far from the coast. Most of his relatives were already there. Aunts and uncles and cousins and sisters— we'd missed the funeral, but we'd arrived in time for the baby.

At lunch, everyone spoke to me, or they nodded and shook me and told me how stout I was. Everyone went out of their way to make me feel welcome. But what I remember feeling is fucking overwhelmed.

I remember everyone wanting to speak to me.

I remember everyone wanting to look at me.

I remember everyone wanting to touch me and asking about my mother and when Jin would give the family another boy and also when all of us would return to Korea.

It wasn't long before I realized that the best answer was no answer at all. It was easier to pretend I didn't know what anyone was saying. So that's exactly what I did.

When Jin's sister asked how I was doing, I smiled.

When his brother asked how old I was, I shrugged.

When a friend of Jin's father asked me where we lived and I didn't answer him, he berated Jin for not teaching me Korean.

Jin heard this, and he winced. Then he turned to me with a look.

But he didn't blame me.

He told everyone that I just didn't know, and I let him.

77.

Ian's family's place in Galveston sits on the coast, nestled on a beach among beaches. The condos beside it are silent, shrouded in darkness. But a pair of chubby Mexican guys sit on the patio below us, blasting a murder mystery podcast, raising their beers at the sight of us

The house itself is pretty modest: there's a bed and some potted plants. Sky-blue walls. A coffee table sits by the television, with kitchen doors leading to a set of windows overlooking the beach.

I've barely shut the door behind me when Ian reaches for my shirt, pulling it over my head. He does it wordlessly, automatically. I let him push me against the wall, pressing himself against me, but then he starts bending me over a counter and I tell him to wait because of course we haven't showered.

Ian looks fucking mortified. There's want in his face. But there's also something closer to need.

So I take his face in my palms.

And I kiss him.

And I let Ian fuck me.

We fuck again, on the mattress.

And as he comes a third time, he keeps grinding into me.

Hey, I say.

Ian slows, but he doesn't stop.

Ian, I say. I don't think it's happening again.

He gives me a look like I've slapped him. But he rolls onto the wood floor. And I collapse beside him, settling my back against the coolness.

Neon porch lights click themselves on, bleeding through the windows. They etch waves across our skin. The two dudes outside open their cooler for more beer.

What's your plan, I say.

What do you mean, says Ian.

You drove us out here, I say. We fucked. So what do you think happens now?

I made a decision, says Ian, scratching his ribs. Like you said. I came back for you.

But you still haven't answered my question.

You need me to say it? After all of this?

You're a single man now, I say.

Yeah, says Ian.

We hear the waves settle against the shore just beyond us. One of the dudes outside burps, chuckling.

I couldn't do it, says Ian. Hiding, you know? Sam said it was fine, and we'd figure something out. Which I think she probably meant. She said we'd figure something out, and she wouldn't tell our families, and I just had to trust her that things would fix themselves. And I wanted to. Like, I really fucking wanted to. But I knew it wouldn't work. I couldn't do that to her, or myself. I felt like I'd rather die, you know? Like I could see the rest of my life, in that one moment, and it was just me being a fucking mess? Fucking depriving myself?

Ian keeps fumbling his hands. I grab one, squeezing his palm.

Does she know where you are now, I say.

I don't know.

Did you tell anyone you were doing this?

No, says Ian. I just came to see you. That's it.

Ian's fingers massage mine. My hands rise to his forearms.

I'm happy for you, I say.

But you know I can't stay here, I say. *We* can't stay here.

Why not, says Ian.

Except there isn't any real weight in his voice. Even if his body doesn't understand, his eyes clearly do.

I want you to do the things that you want to do, I say, but it has to be for *you*. Not because you feel like it's something you should do.

Ian closes his eyes. We're both still lying on the floor. The window's light has shifted, and the glow on our bodies turns pale.

I thought I did, says Ian.

I know, I say.

I really thought this was it, says Ian. Us being together. Like, a proper thing. And I know you wanted this, too. I pretended not to see it, but I knew.

You're right, I say. I did.

Ian doesn't say anything to that. He releases all of the pressure in my hand.

Then he grins.

You're different, says Ian.

I don't think that's what this is, I say.

You wouldn't know, says Ian. Is it someone else?

I look at him. And then I purse my lips.

Yeah, I say. But it's mostly just me.

He puts his head on my thigh. I run my fingers through his hair. We stay like that for a moment.

What the fuck am I doing, says Ian.

The same thing I am, I say. We're figuring it out.

And will you be around, says Ian. While I do?

It'll be different, I say. But if you need me, I'll be there.

Yeah, says Ian. Hey?

Yeah?

Thank you. For coming here.

You basically kidnapped me.

You came consensually. Please don't joke about that.

I have to. For the rest of our lives.

Maybe that'll be what finishes me off.

No, I say. You'll find a handsome someone and settle down.

You think so?

Yeah. And if that doesn't happen, you'll figure something else out. The same way that we all do.

Ian adjusts his head on my leg. I keep my hands on his head. We're both naked, but it's hardly erotic, and it isn't too long before he starts snoring.

The rain starts tapping above us, too. The two sounds blend together.

And it's kind of hilarious: I'd almost forgotten what it sounded like to be caught under the water. You can't hear a single drop in Mae's home, but here, you have to sit through every single one. All you can do is wait for it to end.

78.

At some point on the trip with Jin, I got lost in his sister's house. I ended up on a guest room futon. It was comfortable there. I stayed.

A cousin of mine found me. She was around my age. When she asked if I was okay, I told her I was fine in Korean. She asked if I wanted her to stay, and I told her that was all right, and we spent our afternoon that way. She held my hand, singing softly under her breath.

Eventually, I woke up. My cousin was gone. And Jin sat cross-legged next to me, peeking over my shoulder.

He asked if I wanted to come outside. I told him I didn't.

Okay, said Jin, and then he set his back against the wall beside me.

It's where we spent the rest of the night. The festivities downstairs dragged into the evening. I watched my father until he fell asleep sitting up, slumped over with his arms crossed.

And I wondered what he was dreaming about.

And I wondered what he saw when I stood beside the rest of his family.

The rest of our trip would glide by: the next day, we'd eat breakfast. I'd piddle around with my cousins. We'd set off fireworks. I'd cut my feet in the sand. We'd eat dinner outside.

The adults would drink in a circle.

Jin and I would wave goodbye before we traveled back to Seoul.

But what I remember most vividly is Jin dozing beside me. And the face he made when he woke up. He didn't know where or when he was.

Then he saw me.

His whole face softened.

Tae-ju, he said. Tae-ju.

I thought he was still asleep. So I held my breath.

But then my father smiled, closing his eyes again.

79.

When I wake up, Ian isn't beside me.

Then I turn my phone back on.

There are so many fucking vibrations that I just set it aside.

But there's a note on the coffee table.

It's Ian's handwriting. Which I realize I've never seen before. And, also, that it's beautiful.

The keys are by the door, he wrote.

> *There's a grocer around the corner. It's been there for decades, even through the storms.*
>
> *Order the fish sandwich. Not the boudain plate.*
>
> *I've called you a car back to Houston. It might take a little while, but they're on the way.*
>
> *And I'll call. Eventually.*
>
> *There are some things I need to think about and I need some time.*

But thank you, TJ. I mean it.

Hope everything works out.

I fold Ian's letter, stuffing it in my wallet. Then I reach for an umbrella by the door.

It's still raining along the pier, getting heavier by the minute. But when I step into the grocer, I fill a basket with water and beef jerky and Gatorade and Doritos. There's a lady at the register, and she smiles my way, asking me something in Spanish.

When I widen my eyes, she switches over to English. Her name tag says Ana.

If the rain keeps picking up, she says, you might find yourself stuck here.

Then can I wait for a while, I ask.

As long as you need, says Ana. Might help to buy lunch, too.

What do you have?

What do you need?

I hear the boudain plate's delicious, I say, and the woman smiles, winking.

Some white folks in flip-flops pump gas from the lot. Drenched locals pop in every few minutes, sopping all over the tile. They all give me a once-over, but then they just nod, and when Ana brings my food on a steaming paper tray, she settles into the seat beside me.

You aren't from around here, she says.

How could you tell?

Ana's eyes smile before she says, We don't get too many folks here in the morning.

I'll come back, I say.

Bring your friends, says Ana.

I have one that's from here. He'd love this place.

Yeah?

Yeah, I say, and then, out of nowhere, I start fucking bawling.

A low hiccup gets my shoulders shaking. My tears sop into the food. Ana gives me a long look, passing me some napkins.

And it occurs to me, fully, that I really am alone.

But when I look up again, Ana's still sitting across from me.

She packs my leftovers in a plastic bag. It's too much for one person.

And as she walks me to the door, Ana rubs my back.

Whatever it is that happened, she says, you'll be all right.

You don't even know what's going on, I say.

Sure don't, says Ana. But I see all types here. You wouldn't believe. So I know that whatever you've got going on will settle itself eventually. You'll keep going.

Then she smiles. I tell her I'll come back. The rain outside just continues to ebb and flow.

80.

I'm walking toward the condo when I see it: a tiny little Audi in the parking lot.

Cam's in the passenger seat. A woman I don't recognize is vaping on the driver's side, leaning against the door.

She barely looks up when I call Cam's name.

When he waves, I do, too.

81.

Back in the condo, we form a circle across the rug. I've opened some newspaper sheets, spreading out the rest of the food.

The Black woman sitting between us doesn't say much of anything, picking through the rice and the boudain and the shrimp. She's in a hoodie and sweats, with bangles on her wrists. Cam's worn the same face since he stepped out of the car.

Then Cam looks up, clapping his hands.

TJ, says Cam, this is Bree. Bree, this is—

I know all about TJ, says Bree.

The rain falls even harder. Rattles the room in sheets. Bree's still sifting through the boudain with her fork, and now it's my turn to ignore Cam's stares.

We don't have to make this a thing, says Bree. We'll drive back once the storm clears. Then you two can talk your shit out.

How the fuck did you even know where I was, I ask.

Ian, says Cam.

He called you?

He called the bakery, says Cam. Fati called me. Kidnapping's a crime though, even in Texas.

Calm down, I say. We just needed to talk.

Cam gives me a long look. Then he turns back to the food.

When I thank Bree for making the drive, she looks up at me for the very first time.

Thank *him*, says Bree. Cam insisted. I haven't been to Galveston since I was a kid. Before my brother was born.

Kai, I say.

Yeah, says Bree. He loved the beach. Always talked about getting back to it someday.

The three of us eat silently. A yell erupts from the shore.

Don't feel like you have to say anything stupid, says Bree.

I *wasn't*, says Cam.

Right, says Bree.

Then she turns back to me.

Why did you come out here again, she asks. For a man?

I did it for myself, I say.

Mm, says Bree.

You know, she says, I hated Cam for a long time. Did he ever tell you that?

No, I say.

Of course he didn't, says Bree. But I did. Hated him as much as anything. And I knew it wasn't his fault. There was no reason for the thing that happened to my brother to happen. Life reached out, and it fucking squeezed, and Kai just happened to be in the way. This fucking country will destroy you and there's only so much one person can do. He'd never say this, but I think that's one of the reasons he left Louisiana. And it still caught up with him.

Cam doesn't say anything to this. He just keeps eating, looking down at his food.

But do you know what this fucker does, says Bree. This fucking dummy who was the last person to see my brother alive? This fool? The one person in this fucking world that I think Kai actually loved? He tries burning himself out, fucking and drugging up and down and all over town like a reckless fucking moron, as if he's the only one that's affected. My one link to Kai tried to take himself out of the equation. And that made me even more furious than I already was.

So I came down to tell him that, says Bree. I wanted Cam to hear it from me, after he got out of rehab. And I've seen him every month since. I've come down and made time in my own life to do that.

I look at Cam, but he still won't meet my eyes. He picks at a piece of loose skin on his hand. When I set my palm on it, he stops.

At first he wouldn't see me, says Bree. Like he had a fucking choice. But I insisted.

What did you want him to hear, I say.

Bree looks at me. She smirks.

That destroying himself wouldn't make anything better, says Bree.

That makes Cam cough. I don't have to look at him to see the tears falling down his face.

Kai's dead, says Bree. That's never going to change. But I needed Cam to know that his life wasn't just his own. I needed him to know that there was someone else who fucking cared about him.

But then I pull up this weekend, says Bree, and I see him looking frantic. A little like I was. Then Cam tells me about how you've gone and gotten fucking catnapped.

I wasn't kidnapped, I say.

You were fucking kidnapped, says Bree.

Okay, I say.

So you need to keep this guy close, says Bree, pointing at Cam. Okay?

Okay, I say.

Don't fucking disappear on him, says Bree.

I'll try, I say.

Good, says Bree.

The three of us exhale. We've made our way through most of the food. All that's left are the entrails, and the shells of what was there.

Then Cam says, I think the rain's starting to settle.

It isn't, says Bree.

And she's right. It's another few hours before water stops dancing on the ceiling. When the neighbors below us emerge, they call out to one another in Spanish: they want to know how everyone's holding up, if everyone's okay.

82.

Our ride back to Houston is mostly silent. The storm scared most of the traffic away. Bree's a smooth driver, gliding from one lane to the next, and I slump in the back seat while Cam sits up front.

But the car smells like pot and sage. Bree cracks a window once we're back on the feeder road. It brings in smells of the city, and it isn't much longer before we're back in the Heights, and the bakery looms on the edge of the block. Once Bree parks, I open the door, but Cam stays put up front.

I'm borrowing him for a minute, says Bree.

Aye, aye, I say.

Next time you lose your mind over dick, call your friends first.

I'll try.

Good, says Bree.

Sometimes the best we can do is live for each other, she says. It's enough. Even if it seems like it isn't.

And then she grins.

83

Our register's empty. The counter's clear. I kick my shoes off in the doorway, starting for the stairs—but then I change my mind, heading down the hallway instead.

Mae's bedroom door is shut. I knock before I hear muttering, and then footsteps, and then Mae's hushed whispers.

He can stay in there, I say. It's cool.

Another moment of silence passes. Then the door opens.

Mae's standing in front of me, tying her robe. Ivan's tucked in the bed. He nods, and I wave back.

Hello, stranger, says Mae.

Hey, I say.

I know you're an adult, she says. I can't tell you what to do. And I'm still not sure what happened, but—

I'm sorry, I say. I didn't mean to scare anyone.

Mae blinks at me a few times. And then her shoulders relax.

You haven't apologized in years, she says.

How did it feel, I ask.

I should be asking you that.

Maybe it'll get easier.

Of course it will, says Mae.

Okay, can you talk now?

I can, says Mae. Is something wrong?

No. But I decided what I'm going to do. Or what I'm gonna try to do.

Mae turns back to Ivan. He shrugs, smiling.

We don't have to do this now, I say. I just wanted to let you know.

Okay, says Mae.

She sets a hand on my shoulder, and I see what's on her face. But I wonder how she's really feeling.

Then I say, I just wanted to say thank you.

Mae blinks a few times. She tells me to wait a moment, stepping into the bedroom, riffling through drawers. Ivan chuckles from the bed, drawing the sheets closer around him.

We missed you, he says. Estábamos preocupados, tu sabes?

Verdad, I ask.

Si claro, says Ivan. Es la verdad.

When Mae comes back to me at the door, she's holding a photo. It's folded around the edges. The print's fading from wear.

I've never seen it before.

It must've been from the trip to Korea.

Jin's got his arm around my shoulder. I look like I can't decide what face I want to make. My father's smiling though, throwing a peace sign toward the camera, and I've formed one with my own fingers, too.

Mae presses the photo against my chest until I take it.

Thanks, Ma, I say.

I expect her to flinch, but she doesn't.

Instead, she beams.

You're welcome, son, says Mae.

84.

I text Noel.

    Hey. How are you?

They respond immediately.

    Magical. Are you all right?

    I am.

But, I add, can I see you? So we can talk?
It's another few minutes before they reply.

    I'm a little busy.

    Okay. It's kind of important though?

But five minutes pass.
And then ten minutes.
While I wait, Cam opens my bedroom door. He sinks onto the floor across from me, hugging Mochi, settling onto the carpet in sweatpants.
And this is when Noel texts back.
Except it isn't exactly a text.
All they've done is drop a pin.
So I grab my shoes. I tell Cam not to wait up.

85.

Montrose's traffic isn't much after midnight—just the stragglers leaving the bars, and the locals walking their dogs, and the random cars with busted headlights speeding who fucking knows where.

I pass the Target and the sex shop. And the Shell station and the smoke shops. I pass Niko Niko's and Aladdin and BB's on the corner. I pass the Hollywood corner store and the AutoZone and the tiny Cuban walk-up diner. But it isn't long before I'm parking beside JR's, behind the tiny little torta truck that runs until four in the morning.

Potted plants and tiny trees dot the bar's patio. Everyone lounging looks like a regular. A handful of folks bounce along to some Ariana Grande track by the speakers, nodding and brushing hips and cupping each other's elbows, laughing.

But Noel sits on a bench, pulling on a vape, and they blow a little smoke my way, patting the seat beside them.

I don't know what to tell them.

And I don't know what they're thinking.

So we smoke.

We watch the bar.

Noel's phone buzzes, but they let it ring and ring.

Eventually I say, This tastes like avocado.

That's what it is, says Noel.

Am I right?

Maybe. It's called Berry Blast? But that felt like bullshit.

Look, I say, and Noel turns to face me.

There's no anger or frustration or anything in their expression.

It looks a little like resignation.

Which scares me.

I don't know what to do about that.

So what I say is: Want to dance with me?

As soon as the words leave my mouth, Noel's face cracks.

What, they say.

Don't laugh.

No one's laughing.

Seriously, I say. I mean it.

I thought that wasn't your tea, says Noel.

This song's nice, I say. Slow. I think I can handle it.

Noel tries turning stern again. They purse their lips. But it's too late, and I know that, and they sigh, letting me take their hand, guiding them toward the crowd.

The last person I danced with was Jin. I don't even know where to begin. But the folks alongside us smile our way, slowing their rhythm. And my knees bend a little to match them, until Noel closes the distance between us, just a little, so that our shoulders brush as we bob along.

Then the music turns to something slower. A lilting Patti LaBelle. I reach for Noel, just to see what'll happen, and they give me a look before pressing against my body.

We sashay against each other, keeping time with the bass.

You're not bad, says Noel.

I'm fucking drowning here, I say.

Sometimes that's only what it feels like. You're doing fine.

Look, I say. So. I just wanted to say I'm sorry.

What about, says Noel.

I had to figure something out, I say. There was something I had to take care of.

So that's what you were doing, says Noel.

Yeah, I say.

You don't have to justify anything to me.

But I think I do. And I've wanted to talk to you about this. Because I've just been kind of floating along? It's hard to explain.

Some bar goers behind us start clapping. The guy they're circling around hides his face in his hands. The group counts off numbers, cheering at forty-two, and the birthday dude downs three shot glasses straight from the bar top.

Noel and I clap, keeping time with Patti. Then they turn back to me. And Noel flips around, until their back's against my chest, folding my arms over theirs as we sway.

You were saying, says Noel.

Should I speed up, I ask.

You're doing fine.

Okay, I say. Fuck. I think when you've been in one place long enough, it starts to feel like that's the whole world, you know? Seeing anything beyond it is hard. Like, it doesn't even feel possible? And I think a part of me has been fighting to keep things that way in my life. Uncomplicated and easy. Which I guess is a kind of safety.

Noel drags their sneakers against the concrete. I glide my fingers toward their hips. They reach back toward my dick, squeezing, and when I snort they let go.

Keep going, says Noel.

But that safety's not real, I say. And you lose so much trying to keep it.

So what now, says Noel. Is this you saying you've become a bad boy? Or do we drive off into the sunset?

I'm saying that I want to stop being safe, I say. And I don't know what that looks like. But I think it's okay that I don't know.

And, I say, I think it's okay if you have to go.

But, I say, if you want me to go with you, I will.

Noel cranes their neck, really scrutinizing me. They turn around, again, so that we're facing each other.

That's an interesting development, says Noel.

I know, I say. But I realized I've actually been thinking about this for a while.

We might not work out, says Noel. We *probably* won't, honestly.

You're right.

We might fuck each other over. The sheen might wear off.

It might.

And we might never learn to trust each other. Whatever this is could really fuck us up.

That's a possibility, I say. But not knowing would probably be worse. Because, Noel, I like you. I really do. And I don't like everyone—

You like Cam.

I do. But it's different. You're different.

Hunh, says Noel.

Somehow, the crowd of dancers around us has tripled. Stray cars tumble across the road. Lights in the neighborhood's homes have all gone out, but the shitty Christmas bulbs above us are glowing. They're our only beacons in the dark.

Noel and I bump the bodies beside us, but without losing step with each other. And it feels comfortable. Like we're all swaying together, in the thick of ourselves. Which is when the track above us flips once again, and Tim Maia's voice booms from the speakers, and I don't recognize the song but I can tell from Noel's face that they do. So I let my hips move, just a little bit, and for the first time all evening Noel breaks into the biggest grin. They take that as their cue, bringing me closer to them, until we're moving at the same pace, faster than I ever would on my own.

But it doesn't feel ridiculous.

It feels right.

You're doing great, says Noel.

Ha, I say.

Hey, says Noel. No one's saying that this is forever.

I know, I say.

And we don't need to have everything planned from the jump.

Okay, I say. But what we're doing right now feels nice.

And Noel touches my face, brushing at the fuzz around it.

Good, they say. Then we'll keep doing it as long as it's nice.

And how long is that, I ask, grinning.

Don't ask me to do the work for you, says Noel. We'll figure it out together.

1.

Before I picked Cam up from the rehab clinic in Richmond, I watched him from my car. Just for a minute.

He wandered from end to end of the lobby.

He stared at his phone.

And then he stood still for a long, long minute.

I wondered if he'd walk back inside.

Or call the whole thing off.

I wouldn't have blamed him.

So I called Cam's name, waving him over to my car.

And for the first time in over a decade, he smiled back at me.

86

The Heights are quiet when I pull up again, and the house is silent when I step inside.

I close my eyes, just for a moment, and I think about tomorrow.

And the days afterward.

And what it'll mean to step through a home, in a brand-new place, where my people aren't.

But when I walk into the kitchen, Cam's sitting on a stool, leaning against the counter. He almost looks like he's praying.

I nudge him, and he doesn't move.

So I nudge a little harder.

Then I squeeze his chest and he jolts awake.

Fucker, says Cam.

Come upstairs, I say. You'll hurt your back sleeping down here.

Cam gives me a look. And then he stands, clattering the stool across the floor.

He steps toward the stove. Grabs one thing after another from the fridge. It's all cabbage and bacon and other assorted knickknacks, and I have no idea where he's gotten these things from, and I start to ask what he's doing, and I start to tell him to stop, but I don't do either of those things.

So Cam chops and he minces.

He cracks eggs into a bowl.

He beats dry into wet.

He ladles everything into a pan, watching it sizzle.

When Cam's finished with the dish, he sets it between us, grabbing a pair of chopsticks.

It's a cabbage pancake, layered in sauce and bonito flakes and seaweed powder, stuffed with odds and ends from the fridge.

I take a bite and nearly choke from the heat.

This is *good*, I say.

Bitch, says Cam. Don't sound so surprised.

The two of us chew in the darkness, sharing a plate, leaning against the counter. The only lights around us shine from our phones.

It's something Kai used to make, says Cam. I always made fun of him for it. But he liked that you could use whatever you have on hand. He thought it brought him closer to where he wanted to be.

Cam and I eat in the dark. Occasionally, we clink chopsticks.

Are you still seeing him, I ask. Kai?

Sometimes, says Cam.

Have you told Bree?

No. And I don't think I will. That might just be something that belongs to me. She might have something that belongs to her, too.

But TJ, says Cam, it was hard when he died.

Okay, I say.

Like really, really hard. There was all this attention for a while. He was dead, but people cared. It seemed like something might happen. It wouldn't have made anything better, and he'd have still been gone, but maybe there would be consequences. So that's what I leaned into. Because I had to. And then, after nothing happened, it felt like nothing else was there. Everyone kind of went away. And then there was just this void. So I tried to fill it with whatever. And anything was better than nothing. And I knew it wasn't helping me, but it was still something.

I'm sorry you had to go through that, I say. And that you felt alone.

Yeah, says Cam, well. My fault.

No, I say. It's a thing that happened, and it was horrible. And I'm sorry.

Right, says Cam, and then he grins.

But what I've learned, he says, is that we need everyone. Like, it's a group effort. You and Mae and Noel. And Minh and Diego. And Fati and Jake and Fern and Ivan. And Kai. It takes all of these people to make one person's life okay. One person can't do it for you by themselves. I don't think I ever really understood that, and now I do. It's our responsibility to take care of each other.

He adds: I've always been a little jealous of you. You know?

You had this family, Cam says. You had context. You had history and a road map and a plan. I loved that for you. I admired it. And then, at some point, it made me so fucking upset. I didn't know how to relate to you anymore, you know? So I just stopped calling.

I get it, I say.

It was shitty.

It was fucking horrible. But I'll give you a pass since I'm leaving.

Cam looks up at me, blinking.

He exhales.

Then he snags the pancake's corner, chewing again.

Cute, says Cam.

What, I say. That's it?

Didn't you say no one's ever called you that? It's my moving gift to you.

Cam folds his chopsticks. He leans into the counter.

He says, How are you feeling about Noel?

I don't know what the fuck is happening, I say.

But you're happy?

I think I'm okay.

Good, says Cam. Then I am, too.

I'm gonna fucking miss you, I say.

Whatever, says Cam. Just call.

And Cam stands across from me.

He dips over the counter.

Then he leans into the wood, kissing me on the lips.

And I kiss him back.

We do that for a minute.

Once our teeth gnash together, we separate, laughing.

Fuck, says Cam.

Gross, I say.

And I'm your boss now. Did Mae tell you?

I'm never fucking acknowledging that.

Then I'll fire you. You're fired.

And the two of us sit in the kitchen, chewing across from each other. When there's a screech in the road, I look up at Cam, but he doesn't even flinch.

Don't be scared, says Cam.

I'm not, I say.

Fucking hell, says Cam. What are you going to do out in the world?

Kai, again

A few months after I died, my mother's roses came into bloom. Bree couldn't figure out why. My mother didn't want to speculate. But every few days, she'd moisten their leaves with a spray bottle. Sometimes my mother sang to them. She held her phone in front of her lips, texting me the recordings to a number that never responded.

It happened to Shun, too: one day, the cherry blossoms beside Oda's apartment unfurled. They were officially living together by then. Neither of them could believe it. But eventually, Shun took photos of the flowers, clipping them for his coffee table, which he dutifully sent to my phone every few weeks. The petals grew more and more brilliant every month. Shun never told anyone what he was doing.

Cam saw each of these messages as they arrived. He read them on my phone. And he never replied. But he'd replay my mother's voice from our balcony in LA, flicking through the pictures Shun sent from halfway across the world.

After the first few days, these messages became something to look forward to. If Cam destroyed himself, he'd miss the next week's blossoming. He had to stick around or he wouldn't catch the petals falling in Kansai.

•

In either case, a few more things happened before the end.

The first was something that Cam whispered in my ear. We were walking home from some concert, or a movie, or maybe a party. Our gait was so aligned that we knocked elbows and hips and knees. We giggled every time it happened. Even when we were fighting. Like a pair of fucking children.

When Cam said the words again, I just kept walking.

He stayed silent, too, following after me. But this time from behind.

•

Another day, Cam and I were out in the world again—in the park—and we spotted some kid on his own. He looked aloof in the way that kids can. We were already running late for something, and I remember that it was my fault, but Cam stopped, just for a minute.

Cam stooped down for the boy. Cam asked if he was lost, and the kid said that he was. Cam asked if he lived around here, and the kid said that he didn't. Cam asked the boy if he wanted us to wait with him, but by now the kid was looking at me.

I nodded. The kid nodded, too.

So we stood beside him, poking at our phones.

It was a balmy afternoon. Everyone was outside. Passersby stared at us sometimes, but mostly no one cared. Every few minutes, the kid looked up at Cam, and then at me. When I made a funny face, the boy didn't smile.

. . .

Maybe twenty minutes later, a car honked across the road. A woman waved, squinting at the two of us. We both waved back. And then the kid, without turning our way, began walking toward his mother or his aunt or his sister.

When he made it to the car, he stopped and turned around. He nodded at the two of us exactly once. He yelled, *Good luck*.

•

Another day: We're walking to a theater, a gallery, a nightclub. I'm exhausted from last night's flight from Haneda, but I tag along with Cam because this is the least I can do.

But that's when Cam stops in the middle of the road. He asks if I really want to go.

No, I say. Not really.

Good, says Cam.

He nods toward a boba shop with an open sign and a flickering light. The drink he buys me is neither sweet nor sour—it's some pleasant hybrid in the center. A third way.

•

Another day: Cam repeated those three words under his breath. We were fucking. And then we weren't. He stopped, waiting for me to speak. But I grabbed his dick, pushing him back in—and Cam came immediately, gasping underneath me.

Afterward, lying beside each other, he asked if that was my response.

•

Cam asked what I was doing for Christmas, and I told him I'd be in Kansai. He took the news with a smile. This was something we hadn't talked about: my being elsewhere for these stretches of time, and how that fit into the life we were making together.

When I asked if he wanted to come along, Cam asked *why* I was asking. Was it because I wanted to? Or because I thought he wanted me to?

I said, Whichever answer is correct.

Thankfully he was a good traveler. From the flight to Taipei, to our connection in Narita, to the train we took to Osaka, Cam was all silence and smiles. He didn't lose his passport. Didn't interrupt when I purchased tickets, or bought food, or received change. Whenever he needed to piss, he accomplished that quickly and efficiently, waved at the kids in the aisle who stared him down on the bullet train.

We stayed with Shun and Oda, unpacking our bags in the guest room. Cam touched everything inside their apartment: the walls, the doors, the floor, the tatami mats. He knocked twice on their coffee table. He grasped at the bookshelf. Outside, he rubbed the fallen pollen between his fingers.

Shun walked us around his neighborhood, and then to the market in Tennōji, and then to the shrine. I stood with Oda while Shun talked Cam's head off. The grilling was broken up by laughter, but I wasn't sure how that made me feel.

When we made it to the shrine, I asked Cam if he wanted to pray with us. He shook his head once. But he watched us bow, clap, and bow. When I turned around, he was taking a photo for a trio of women, angling their phone to fit them all into the frame.

Eventually, Shun found a moment to corner me. He said, *I don't see the problem.*

I told Shun that this is precisely the issue: the problem with people is usually the thing we can't see.

We spent New Year's Eve at a gay bar in Doyama. The four of us slurped soba over beer, yelling into one another's ears. When the countdown began, everyone in the room screamed in their languages, and I heard Japanese and Mandarin and English and French and Portuguese and Korean and Spanish and German. Once the ball dropped, the men around us started to kiss. But Cam only touched my face with his fingers, smiling.

And then, the weekend before we returned to LA, the four of us went to an onsen. I couldn't imagine what we looked like to its owners. But they ushered us inside regardless, waving at our backs.

We shuffled from the building's sitting room to its dining room to its bath. Cam looked tentative at first, but then he sank into the water. Oda made small talk beside him. I lazed next to Shun, closing my eyes. We blew bubbles from our noses, willing the moment into something longer.

The four of us shared a room. Laid our tatami mats side by side. And it wasn't long before Shun and Oda started snoring, but then I heard Cam rustling, standing to leave the room. I waited a few more minutes before I followed, shutting the door behind me.

I didn't spot Cam outside. And I didn't find him around the building's corner. When I passed the matron in the hall, I bowed lightly, and she smiled. She asked how my stay was going, and I told her it was fine.

It's a lovely night, she said. *We're lucky to have it.*

. . .

I took one circle around the building, and then another, before I found him on the bridge smoking. Cam didn't say a word as I approached. But he offered me a cigarette, and I took it.

We smoked through the whole pack. Below us, the bridge held a view of the entire onsen. In the building across from us, we watched a group of women drinking sake in a circle on the roof. They laughed at one another, leaning into each other's shoulders.

The next morning, Cam and Oda wheeled our suitcases toward the train when Shun grabbed my elbow. He asked where we'd wandered in the middle of the night. I told him, and he folded his lips.

Shun said, *It's rare to find someone who'll follow you.*

•

A few months later, I flew to Houston but I didn't tell Cam.

When I got to the airport, I took a Lyft straight through the city. I tried seeing it the way Cam had told me, but I didn't know what to look for. Houston looked endless. Borderless. I wasn't sure whether it held possibility or nothing at all.

I dropped my bag off at the hotel, and I sat on the bed. When I went downstairs, TJ was waiting for me, playing with his thumbs.

When I waved, he waved back, snorting.

I thought, Duh. That's where he got it from.

. . .

We didn't say much to each other in TJ's car. Didn't have much in common aside from the one thing. But TJ looked comfortable with himself. When a pickup truck in front of us slammed on its brakes, he didn't even crease his eyebrows, maneuvering alongside it.

The restaurant he brought me to was homier than I expected. There wasn't a menu. They didn't serve alcohol. TJ spoke to the server in Korean, shrugging, and the woman nodded afterward, smiling at me.

So, said TJ. You really came down.

I told you I would.

Sure. But you really did it.

The two of us stared at each other. I sipped the water in front of me.

I just don't know what to give him, I said.

So we're getting right to it, said TJ. And you think *I* know.

I think you know Cam best.

We haven't spoken in years.

He talks about you. You mean a lot to him.

TJ looked up at me then. His mouth hung open, just a little bit.

Well, said TJ. He's a fucking handful.

He said that about you, too.

Cam knows what to think about everyone but himself.

But you're lucky to have each other.

If you say so.

The guy bussing our table set our drinks in front of us. Neither of us moved. Then TJ reached across the table, folding his fingers.

You must really love him, said TJ. To come all the way down here and find me.

Yeah, I said. I don't know what to make of it.

You flew a long way, said TJ. So I'll tell you this story. A little while after

Cam left Houston, we had a falling out. This was some years ago. It started off as something stupid, but both of us let it fester. We just didn't talk. And eventually it was easier to stop talking altogether. But you probably already know that.

It's come up, I said.

Right, said TJ. Something happened before that though.

I was fucking a lot of guys then, said TJ. Like a lot. Which is fine. I had fun and I was coping and those were some of the best nights of my life. But, you know, some days it was two or three, and other weekends it was twelve, and I wasn't always safe. I knew better, but whatever. I couldn't bring myself to care. Except there was one week where I hadn't been sleeping around, but I'd gotten really, really sick. Totally out of nowhere. It took me out for maybe two weeks, and I spent most of that on the toilet. So my dad made me go to a doctor, which I hadn't done in years, and I passed by this clinic and they ran some tests and the first nurse brought another nurse in the room to ask if I knew I was poz.

TJ kept the same tone of voice as he spoke. It didn't rise or fall. When our waiter dropped by our table, TJ smiled until he left again.

I already knew about the meds, said TJ. I knew that if you're undetectable, you're untransmissible. I knew my life wasn't over. But this was still a fucking buzzkill, to say the least. I was already stuck in fucking Houston. I still lived with my fucking parents. I didn't have a plan, and now there was this new complication, too. This other thing on my back.

Sounds like a lot, I said.

Yeah, said TJ. So I was in a bad place.

And, said TJ, the one person I wanted to tell wasn't around. He was actually graduating that week in New York, with a degree in finance, and I didn't want to dampen his news with my shit, right? So I didn't say anything about it. But when we talked on the phone, Cam could tell something was wrong. I don't know how. And then I told him about my test results like it wasn't a big deal, and then I didn't hear from him for two days.

I thought he was ghosting me. Like, maybe he just didn't want to deal with it. I tried not to think about that, but it was the worst fucking feeling. And then, a few afternoons later, there's this banging on the bakery door, and Cam's sprinting inside with a duffel and bags of takeout.

He'd skipped his graduation for a flight back to Houston. I told him he was being a bitch and a fool. And Cam said, Fine, whatever, I guess, but he stayed with me for the next two weeks. He cooked all my meals. We slept in the same bed. Some afternoons, we just sat in the neighborhood's pool for hours and hours. He got me through one of the hardest times in my life and he did that shit for absolutely nothing in return.

I played with my hands while TJ spoke. I could hardly even look at him. Then he reached across the table, folding my palm into his.

So here's my advice, he said. Just keep him close. That's it. No one has loved me harder than Cam. No one has accepted me as quickly, or as unchangingly. And fucking no one has hurt me harder than that stupid faggot either.

But there's no one in this world that I trust more, said TJ. That's how I feel about your boyfriend.

TJ dropped me off just outside my hotel. I asked if he wanted a beer in the lobby, but he told me he had to get going.

I wake up early, said TJ. Maybe I'll catch you guys in LA. If you stick it out.

You just might, I said.

But listen, I said, can you do me a favor?

I can't imagine what that could possibly be, said TJ.

If Cam ever needs you, I said, can you be there for him?

TJ gave me a long look. He crossed his arms.

He might not, I said. This could be nothing, in the grand scheme of things. But if Cam ever calls, can you answer? Is that something you can do?

The hotel's concierges stood in a circle, laughing into their phones. The sun had fallen. Signage glowed around us. And TJ glowed under that light.

Then he looked up at me, smiling.

And then he walked back to his car.

•

I'd told Cam when I was flying back to California, but I gave him the day after my arrival. The night I landed, back at my place, I sat in the tub for a few hours. Kept my head under the water. So I didn't hear him put his key in the lock, or when he set his shoes at the door, or when he stood in front of the bathroom door.

When I finally looked up, I saw Cam. He held some sunflowers, nestled in a pair of mason jars.

Cam stared at me for a long moment. Then he started stripping in the doorway. And he set one foot in the bathtub, sloshing water onto the mat, and I laughed at him, and Cam laughed, too, and he leaned across the tub, wrapping his arms around me.

I said the three words so quietly that I thought he might have missed them.

But Cam flinched. And then he softened.

•

The weather in Los Angeles feels brisk in spring. In Osaka, the air's a little lighter. Stray cats by Shun's apartment congregate under the trees. But in Baton Rouge, it's about the time that Bree starts pruning her garden. That's a part of her routine: she and my mother will walk around the block, crouching in the plot and sifting their hands through the soil. They work quietly, knowing exactly when to look up at each other and laugh.

. . .

Occasionally Bree turns to the sky, all of a sudden. I've thought about asking her what that means. But I don't need to know. Some things are best kept to ourselves.

•

When I look at Cam now, he seems a little less bewildered. A little less like someone that the world has simply happened to.

This is a good thing.

There are so few of them.

And I want him to hold on to it. Just *being* is the gift I'd like to give him.

Lately, for me, everything is all at once and not at all. It's all very loud and quiet. I've tried explaining this to Cam, but it's tricky.

Then again, understanding is overrated.

Instead, I tell him: Wanna hear what I've learned before I leave?

You aren't going anywhere, says Cam.

And you've gone out of your way to make it so. But I think I've had my fill.

It's well past midnight. Cam's sitting in boxers and a tank top, holding a cat on the back porch. A breeze ruffles his shorts, but he doesn't seem cold.

It doesn't matter what I do, says Cam. You're a part of me. You'll always be a part of me.

So you get it, I say.

Yes, says Cam. That's how it goes. Ad infinitum. With every single person we touch, we're leaving parts of ourselves. We live through them. I thought that was bullshit and I was wrong, because it isn't.

Sure, but—

And you know what? I'm fucking grateful for that. It's horrible, but I'm grateful.

Okay, that's enough—

I'll take it. The memories. Who you were then. Who you've become now. I'll keep as much as I can. For however long it's there for me. And—

Shut up, I say. Shut the fuck up. Shut up, shut up, shut up. Okay? I hear you. I get it. But listen—have you eaten?

ACKNOWLEDGMENTS

Thu

Caro and Brian

Paul

Kalsang

Phil

Nicole

Carlos

Anthony

Ryan

Kevin

Yu

Wei-Qiang

Rumaan

Chau and BJ

Aaron

Ocean

Willing

Na

The SFPL West Portal Team

The Riverhead crew

Susan

Lavina

Nora Alice

Bianca

Hannah

Grace

Katie

Szilvia

Alice

Laura

Ashley

Danielle

Lou

RESOURCES

For info, assistance, and guidance on mental health and mental illness, please check out the following support systems and resources:

Anxiety and Depression Association of America
adaa.org

Black Aids Institute
blackaids.org

Legacy Community Health
legacycommunityhealth.org

National Eating Disorders Association
nationaleatingdisorders.org

National Queer and Trans Therapists of Color Network
nqttcn.com

Not Alone Cafe
notalonecafe.jp

Overeaters Anonymous
oa.org

San Francisco Community Health Center
sfcommunityhealth.org

Trans Lifeline
translifeline.org

The Trevor Project
thetrevorproject.org